Murder Over Fences

Murder Over Fences
A Riley Press Publication
Eagle, MI 48822
rileypress@yahoo.com

Front cover photo by Maddie Operacz
Catalpa leaf: All Threes Leaves by Creazilla
Jumping horse image in Catalpa Farm logo: OpenClipart-
 Vectors from Pixabay
Catalpa Farm logo designed by Margaret Krusinga
Rileydog logo by Tina Evans
Graphics consulting Tina Evans and Margaret Krusinga

Edited by HHC Consulting Group, Jan Durkee, Jan Hall, and Margaret Krusinga

Thanks to Bob Muladore, Tuebor Books, and to Carrie Thorne for their advice and counsel.

Copyright © 2024 Loraine Hudson

All rights reserved.

No part of this book may be reproduced or transmitted in any form or by any means, electronic or mechanical, including photocopying, recording, or by any information storage and retrieval system, without written permission from the publisher.

This is a work of fiction. All characters and situations appearing in this work are fictitious. Any resemblance to real persons, living or dead, or personal situations is purely coincidental.

Have you read the *Beale Street* mystery series also by Loraine Hudson?

House on Beale Street

Stars Over Beale Street

Bones on Beale Street

Fields on Beale Street

Ghost on Beale Street

Storm on Beale Street

Available on Amazon.com in paperback or Kindle format!

Chapter One

"C'mon girl," I crooned. "C'mon Esther."

I held my mare's hoof firmly but gently in my cupped hands and guided it toward the bucket of warm water and Epsom salt on the floor of her stall.

"You want this abscess to go away, don't you?" I asked her. Esther turned her curious gaze in my direction and flicked her ears toward me, as if she knew what I was talking about, and maybe she did. She heaved a patient horsey sigh and started to lower her foot.

Her hoof was inches from the water when I felt her leg stiffen. I patted her shoulder. "C'mon," I repeated. "It won't hurt." But Esther ignored my reassurances. A sound had captured her attention, and she was on high alert. She threw her head up and looked toward the front of the barn, ears pricked. I peered toward where she was looking. All seemed quiet to my inferior human ears, so I gave her foot another slight tug. "Down you go ..."

And down her foot went, stomping into the warm water, spraying it into my face and onto my t-shirt, and soaking my jeans. The bucket flew against the wall and Esther whirled toward her stall door, nearly knocking me over, her eyes bulging and her nostrils flared wide.

She blew out her breath in an explosive snort, a horse's danger warning.

"Easy, Esther. Settle down," I murmured. I put a calming hand on her neck and stood next to her, looking down the barn aisle. But I still heard and saw nothing so, sighing, I bent and retrieved the bucket. I looked ruefully at my sodden shirt and jeans. "Really, Esther. This isn't helpful. I need to—"

And then my ears caught the noise that had alerted my horse. It sounded as if someone was riding at a fast gallop toward the barn, a foolhardy move at best, as a horse running for home can easily get out of control. I knew the people in my stable would know better, so it was more likely a horse had bolted or there was some emergency.

I reached over the stall door and pulled up the latch, slid hurriedly into the aisle, tossed the empty bucket aside, and shut Esther in.

Then I ran toward the barn door to look outside, wondering what in the world was going on. Esther let out a bugling whinny and circled in her stall, kicking up sawdust and loose hay.

"Easy, Esther," I called over my shoulder, but she ignored me—no surprise there.

I burst out of the barn and looked around. The hoofbeats were closer now, and very uneven. Whatever horse it was, it was running lame.

I knew Joe Beers had been out with his Dutch warmblood horse, Donagin, on the cross-country jump course. And as far as I knew, all the other horses were safe in their paddocks. I didn't take the time to do a nose count. Instead, I scrambled around the corner of the barn and stared up the lane to the jump course. Sure enough, there was Donagin charging out of the woods, galloping for home with one front foot barely hitting the ground.

And no rider on his back.

"Cameron! Cameron!" I shrieked, hoping the sound would reach my husband who was in the house studying for another of his never-ending law school exams. I was sure there was no way he could hear me, but I called anyway, just in case.

Moments later Donagin had thundered up to me, wild-eyed, sides heaving, and his coat dark with sweat. I grabbed the reins before he could slip past, gave him a quick stroke on his nose, and pulled him into a paddock. Then I took thirty seconds to slip off his bridle, latched the gate to the enclosure, and took off for the field.

I hoped Donagin wouldn't choose to roll and wreck his saddle, but finding Joe was more important. I sprinted up the lane.

"Joe! Joe!" I yelled. "Joe!"

There was no answer.

The lane leading to the cross-country course ran alongside another outdoor jump course, and beyond that was the arena, its newly-painted jumps shining in the summer sunshine. By the time I reached the end of the lane, I had a stitch in my side and my breath was burning in my lungs. I was no sprinter. I hoped I'd run across Joe hiking for home pretty quickly or I was going to have to go for help and possibly bring our side-by-side utility vehicle out, rather than searching on foot. Cameron and I had bought 120 acres of land, along with the outbuildings and house, to start Catalpa Farm. It was a big plot with a lot of ground to cover, and Joe could be almost anywhere.

I decided to head for the wooded part of the cross-country course. Pausing at the trail, I stopped to listen for anything—the curse of an unseated rider, a call for help, even a groan—but I heard nothing save the rustle of leaves, the occasional call of a sparrow, and my own breathing, which sounded like a pair of bellows. It was hard to hear anything over my panting.

"Joe!" I yelled again. "I've got Donagin in a paddock. He's fine." He wasn't fine, but that was a problem for later. "Where are you?" I added as if we were having a conversation, except we weren't. I heard no reply.

I told myself I shouldn't be surprised that he didn't answer. It was likely he couldn't hear me. I was just at the edge of the woods, and the jump course wound all the way to the back fence, a good half mile.

To be truthful, the persistent silence was scaring me. There was something so *silent* about it. As if no one were here at all. But someone *was* here. Joe Beers was somewhere—perhaps trying to limp back to the barn; perhaps sitting and waiting for help. Joe was an experienced rider, and he always wore a helmet and safety vest. He knew his horse would run for home if he fell off, and also how to take care of himself if he was hurt. It would be okay. I just needed to find him.

I jogged down the first cross-country trail, skirting a brush jump I'd carefully constructed, and I called loudly.

Nothing.

I began to run again and made it down the rest of the east-west trail before I had to walk to catch my breath. I debated cutting through the woods, but the underbrush was so thick that I feared it would slow me down.

I paused to dial Cameron on my cell, but he didn't answer. I left a voicemail asking him to ring me back right away and, stifling my frustration, I hurried on, searching and shouting. *I should've brought the side-by-side*, I thought. *Why didn't I?* My first instinct had been to run out here on foot. It was a bad plan. I needed wheels.

The ditch and a low log jump were ahead. I took a quick look into the hollow, my heart in my throat. No one was there.

"Joe! Joe!" I cried.

Only the sparrows answered.

I stopped to take stock. What if I'd missed him? What if Joe were right now striding along the lane toward the barn, and here I was out in the woods yelling my head off.

I began to run again and turned another corner on the bridle path. I'd check the last jump, a ramp—a wooden structure with a flat face I'd constructed about a month ago—and then I'd head back. If Joe hadn't shown up yet, I'd get Cameron and we'd come out in the side-by-side. Together, we'd find Joe and when we did, we could give him a ride to the barn.

I raced up to the ramp, checked the near side, and then ran around to the back.

There was Joe.

It took me only a split second to realize that Joe wasn't going to be walking back to the barn, or even hitching a ride in the side-by-side today or anytime.

He lay on his stomach in an awkward tumble, his face turned away. All around him, the earth was torn and tossed, and one of his boots was almost buried in the soil. He'd been wearing his helmet and safety vest, but those protective devices hadn't helped him.

His head was turned and his neck twisted at an angle no one's should ever be.

I scrambled over to him, my heart pounding. I knew not to touch him, but I went around to his other side and bent toward his still body, unable to believe what I knew to be true. To my horror, I looked directly into his staring, lifeless eyes.

Gasping, I stood up straight, the woods swimming around me. Struggling to get my equilibrium, I clasped one hand over my mouth. Then I pulled out my phone, dialed 9-1-1, and began to trudge back toward the barn.

I still hadn't heard from Cameron, and someone was going to have to meet the ambulance and direct them back here.

Chapter Two

I found out later that Cameron had left the house to run a couple of errands and stop by the party store to pick up an energy drink to keep from falling asleep over his studying. He had left his phone on his desk, which was why I couldn't reach him.

His car pulled into the driveway just as the ambulance and other emergency vehicles were rolling out of the field, lights flashing. I'd watched the EMTs load Joe's still body onto a stretcher, given the police my statement, and then driven the side-by-side shakily back to the barn, my stomach churning and my teeth clenched so tightly that my jaw ached.

Cameron leaped from his car, his face taut with alarm, and ran across the farm circle drive to enfold me tightly in his arms. "Are you all right?!" he cried, simultaneously patting me on the back and looking over his shoulder at the departing ambulance. "What's going on?"

"Oh, Cameron!" I began to sob against his shoulder. "It's Joe."

"Joe?"

"Joe Beers. He fell off out on the cross-country course. I looked all over for him and couldn't find him, but then I did, and he's ... he's dead, Cameron. I think his neck is broken."

Cameron pushed me slightly away and looked down at me, his eyes wide. "Dead? Joe Beers? The guy with that ..." his eyes fell on Donagin, standing three-legged in his paddock. "... with that Dutch horse? Isn't that him over there?"

I looked over my shoulder. Cameron was no horseman. He wouldn't know a Dutch warmblood horse from an Akhal-Teke, a rare Turkish breed, but he'd heard me talk, and he knew the people and horses to whom I was leasing stalls. And yes, Donagin was a Dutch horse.

"Yes," I quavered. "That's the one."

"Are you sure Joe's dead?" Cameron asked. "Was he wearing his safety vest?"

I gave a small smile through my tears. My man knew his horse lingo. "Yes, he was wearing his vest, but when he fell off he must've ... I don't know, twisted or something. The coroner said it looked as if Donagin fell, too, and maybe landed on him." I put my hands against Cameron's chest and gave him a gentle push. "I've got to call the vet for Donagin. He's injured."

Cameron dropped his arms and put a comforting hand on my shoulder as I phoned Ellis Equine Clinic. I knew Crystal would be at the Keystone Horse Exhibition showgrounds, but she'd come over for me if I phoned, and this was an emergency.

If Donagin had broken something, there might be two deaths on my farm this day. I felt fresh tears running down my face and Cameron tightened his fingers.

I left a voicemail for Crystal and turned to Cameron. "I need to go tend to Donagin. I ran out to find Joe and didn't take time to put him away. I didn't even take his saddle off because I had to meet the ambulance. Poor guy. I'm afraid ..." I let my voice trail off.

While we hurried toward Donagin's paddock, I phoned Elsa Kurchner, Joe's emergency contact, and left a voicemail for her as well. Someone was going to need to decide about next steps with Donagin once the vet looked him over.

The emergency personnel had called Elsa, too, and given her the awful news. When she got the message about Joe, I was sure Joe's horse would be the last thing on her mind. It was no wonder she hadn't answered.

But it wasn't the last thing on my mind. I had to talk to her, despite the awful circumstances. If it turned out that Donagin was catastrophically injured, I had to know what the owner's wishes were. Donagin was a valuable animal. There would probably be an insurance claim at the very least.

I'd opened Catalpa knowing that I would be taking responsibility for a lot of high-end horses. My farm was adjacent to the Keystone Horse Exhibition showgrounds, home to a string of prestigious equine events that ran from spring through fall. The KHE Special, which featured a variety of jumping contests, was approaching and it lasted for over a month. Horses from all over the state and country, and even some international competitors, traveled in for the event. It was the biggest summer show of the year.

Catalpa was meant to stable horses that would benefit from a quiet atmosphere or different facilities for training and show practice, a welcome escape from the hustle and bustle of the showgrounds. It was one of the selling points of my budding business venture.

"I'll help with Donagin," Cameron said as we approached the stricken horse. My husband put his arm across my shoulders.

I frowned. "I feel bad. You probably should be studying, right?"

Cameron made a face. "Civil procedure can wait. If I have to read one more analysis of jurisdiction and venue I'm going to ..." I looked at him. "... fall sound asleep, I guess," he finished.

"You're never going to get to be a famous lawyer and support me and my failing farm if you don't make it through law school," I half joked, wishing I really thought it was a joke.

"Your farm isn't failing. It's just getting started, and I'll make it through just fine," he said. I wasn't so sure about the farm, but I had no doubts about Cameron. My husband was one of the most brilliant people I'd ever met, and the most determined. Once he'd set his mind to finish law school, law didn't stand a chance.

But for now, Donagin.

Donagin was a beautiful, leggy bay with a crooked blaze and one hind stocking, elegant and showy, sweet-tempered and talented, and ... expensive. Really expensive.

I felt my heart drop. What had I gotten myself into, thinking I could care for these equine treasures and their wealthy owners? I hadn't even made it through one show season, and I'd already had a major disaster. What if someone sued me? *I must have been mad to think I could do this,* I thought desperately. I'd risked not only myself, but Cameron, who was trying his best to start a career.

And Joe.

Joe Beers, the first person to take a gamble and board at Catalpa rather than at the Keystone show grounds, was dead. Dead after going over one of the jumps I'd built, on my property. At a farm that hadn't even been open a year. Joe was a good guy and a superb horseman. He didn't deserve that fate.

If I hadn't needed to attend to an injured horse, I would have collapsed onto the gravel and cried my eyes out. But I had a job to do. It was time to do it. I squared my shoulders, grateful for Cameron's steady presence next to me.

Donagin dropped his muzzle into my hand when I opened the paddock gate and Cameron stepped back to let me walk through. I gave the horse a pat on the shoulder and eyed with trepidation the injured foreleg. He was putting no weight on it at all, and his body was peppered with cuts and scrapes. The ankle was already beginning to swell. Not a good sign.

I unbuckled the saddle and swung it over the paddock fence, giving Cameron a wan smile when he picked it up and carried it toward the tack room in the barn.

"Thanks," I called. "If you can find the saddle cover, would you put it on?"

"You got it."

"Would you also grab Donagin's halter and lead? They're hanging on his stall."

"Sure," Cameron called and disappeared into the barn.

I patted Donagin's shoulder and, crooning to him, ran my hand down the injured leg, pausing at the fetlock and touching gentle fingers over the joint. There was heat there, and even the light pressure caused the horse to jerk his foot upward. But like the well-trained gentleman that he was, he didn't move away, and he let me cup the hoof in my hand to inspect his injury.

Nor did he shy when my phone rang and, to my

relief, I saw it was Ellis Equine Clinic calling.

I let go of Donagin's foot and put the phone to my ear.

"Hey, Annie. You called. What's up?"

"Crystal. Thank God," I said, trying to keep my voice from shaking.

Chapter Three

Crystal Ellis, Equine Veterinarian.

Crystal and I had been fast friends from elementary through high school in Philadelphia, but lost touch when we departed for college. Then, in a welcome twist of fate, we'd both ended up back in our home state—in the same town, no less. Crystal had her equine practice, and I was trying my darndest to start my Catalpa Farm venture.

Crystal was dedicated and highly skilled, with an equine medical specialty. I knew if there was anything to be done for Donagin, she'd do it.

She left her truck in the Catalpa parking area and hurried over to Donagin's paddock, gazing gravely at his injured leg. She looked the horse over carefully, exclaiming at the long cuts and abrasions. Then she took x-rays and did an ultrasound of the wounded limb, moving carefully yet quickly to determine the scope of his injuries.

I waited with bated breath as she examined the x-rays, and then called me over to see. To my immense relief, she said that Donagin had not broken any bones. He had, however, torn a tendon in his left front ankle and was going to be out of commission for a while—likely up to six months. He'd be on strict stall rest for a few days, then he would need to be slowly hand-walked. He could have no unmanaged exercise, and only controlled slow riding once it was clear how well he was progressing. Would he return to full soundness? It depended on how his rehab went. The tear was serious, and there would be scar tissue, so another tear was possible if he started back to work too early or had another mishap.

Donagin was definitely out of the business of showing in the KHE, although who would have ridden him even if he hadn't been injured, I had no idea. Joe was his owner and trainer, and so far as I knew the only person who might have shown him.

The cuts and scrapes on Donagin's legs would heal but would need watching and tending. "This poor fellow must've had a time of it," Crystal said, rubbing Donagin's nose. She had helped me move Donagin into a stall, where he stood forlornly in the corner. "He's one banged-up guy." Crystal ran a hand gently down the front of one of Donagin's legs. "These scrapes? They almost look like contact burns. I wonder if he hit the top of the ramp?"

I frowned. "It's a low jump. Donagin can jump much, much higher."

Crystal nodded. "Right. It's curious. He looks as if he took a wrong step, and down he went." She glanced at me. "And his rider was killed?"

I grimaced and tried not to think about Joe's lifeless eyes. "Yes."

Crystal shook her head. "What a tragedy. You must be beside yourself." She touched me lightly on the shoulder.

My breath caught and I couldn't answer right away, so Crystal pulled out her tablet and began to enter her notes while I pulled myself together. She wrote up detailed instructions for Donagin's care and sent them off to me via email, and prescribed a low dose of reserpine, a sedative to keep him quiet in his stall. Then, as she was loading her equipment to leave, my phone rang. A distraught Elsa Kurchner identified herself, which was a good thing, because my brain felt as if it had turned to mush. I'd already forgotten the name of the person on Joe's emergency paperwork.

"How is he? How is Donagin?" she wailed. "Joe loved him, and he had such hopes. Now he'll never ride again."

I felt my stomach drop to the tips of my toes.

"I'm so sorry," I said, and had to wait out a storm of weeping. When Elsa had composed herself, she asked again about Donagin's injury, asked if he could stay at Catalpa while he rehabbed, and asked if she could pay me for the extra care.

I turned the offer of payment down, although I probably should have taken the money. It wasn't as if Catalpa was doing anything except going farther in the hole at the moment, and when the news got out about Joe's death, I wondered if I'd ever have any other boarders. What if people decided Catalpa was unsafe, or unlucky?

I didn't want Catalpa to be impacted by the disaster today, but at the same time, a man was dead. I hadn't caused it, and I did not think there was a dark cloud hanging over Catalpa. Yet, the tragedy had occurred on my farm. On my "watch," so to speak. I felt guilty for worrying about Catalpa. It seemed self-centered under the circumstances.

I realized Elsa was talking and I quickly tuned in, hoping I hadn't missed anything important.

"I want to thank you," Elsa was saying shakily, "for acting so quickly and finding Joe. The doctor said there was nothing anyone could have done, but ..." she paused to gain control of her voice again, "I wanted you to know that."

My selfish heart drew a deep sigh of relief. I'd wanted to start a farm like Catalpa since I was a kid, and to have it end like this would be heartbreaking. Fortunately, it didn't sound as if Elsa was going to hold me responsible for any sort of negligence. I shoved my own emotions aside. A man is dead, I told myself for the fiftieth time. Stop thinking about yourself.

"I'll let you know about the arrangements for Joe," Elsa went on. "We'll have a service down here in Miami. Perhaps you could spread the word at the showgrounds? I don't know if anyone would travel that far, though."

"I'd be glad to. Just send me the details. Do you mind me asking ..." I hesitated. "What is your—um—relationship to Joe?"

Daughter? Niece? Lover?

Elsa gave a brief laugh that ended in a gulp. "I'm his wife," she said, and I immediately felt embarrassed.

He'd never mentioned Elsa and she didn't share Joe's last name. Nor had he identified her as his spouse on his emergency paperwork or on the board agreement. But then, I'd never shared any particular confidences with Joe Beers. I'd liked him. He was friendly and easy-going. He had a lovely horse. He was entered at KHE. He was leasing a stall at Catalpa. He paid on time. He always rode with safety equipment. That was it. All I knew about him.

"We haven't been married very long," Elsa went on. "Only about six months. I planned to join him ..."

Again, she struggled to get her voice under control. "I had planned to join him in about a week. I was going to finish up something here in Florida, then fly up before the show started."

"I'm so sorry," I said again.

I realized belatedly that Crystal was standing by her truck waiting for me to finish my call, and I asked Elsa if she could hang on. I muted my phone and walked over to talk to Crystal.

"I'm going to go," my friend said. "I'll check Donagin again tomorrow. Stall rest and that's it for now. We'll move on to hand-walking, depending on how things progress. Anti-inflammatories. I'll ultrasound him again in about five days."

"Okay," I said weakly, wondering if Elsa realized what the bill was likely to be for Donagin's veterinary care. Multiple visits, ultrasounds, x-rays, yikes. But I wasn't going to bring it up for now. Joe's wife had enough on her plate, and the Catalpa credit card had a little leeway. A little.

"Cameron doing okay?" Crystal asked quickly.

"Yes, he's inside studying."

"Call me later," Crystal said, and I nodded.

I put the phone back up to my ear and took it off mute. "Sorry. Just saying goodbye to the vet. Don't worry about Donagin. I'll make sure he's well taken care of."

"When he can be transported, I'll make arrangements to get him to the stable where he usually stays down here in Florida," Elsa said. "And make sure you send me any bills."

Sweet lady, I thought, and said, "I will. If there's anything I can do ..."

"Thank you. I'm waiting to hear when they'll send him h-h-home ..." There was a long pause, and I heard Elsa struggling to control her weeping.

"I'd like to attend the memorial," I said. "Keep me posted."

"I will." Elsa clicked off.

I took a deep breath and went back to Donagin's stall. He was still standing in the corner, weight off his left forefoot. Crystal had given him the sedative to keep him quiet, and his eyes looked at me sleepily.

"I'll take care of you, fella, till we know what's going to happen next," I told him, and threw him a flake of hay to munch on.

It was nearly time to do chores, but there was still Esther, waiting patiently in her stall for me to attend to the abscess in her foot. That had to come first, although I knew at least one of the horses was likely to object strongly to his dinner being delayed.

I shrugged, found the bucket I had thrown aside, drew more warm water, added Epsom salt, and recommenced soaking my horse's hoof.

Esther, jockey club name "Almost Esther," was a retired thoroughbred racehorse. She'd only raced three times, apparently deciding that tearing around a track trying to run faster than her horsey friends and allies was far more work than she was willing to expend. She was just too quiet to be a successful racehorse, actually one of the things that drew me to her.

Thoroughbreds have the reputation of being rather hot, although often that's undeserved. They're on edge and tuned up from being on the track, but if they're given a good letdown period after being raced, they can be as manageable as any other horse. I had wanted a quiet horse, and she seemed as if she was just the one for me.

Also, Esther was a solid bay without a bit of white

on her. I've always had a soft spot for horses like that.

I'd picked up Esther for a song, and if I could get her sound—she'd had a trailer accident on the way to Catalpa, and then developed this dumb hoof abscess—I intended to do some showing myself. Maybe at one of the Keystone venue's less high-end events.

Esther was a made-for-dressage mare once I could get some training miles on her. And one thing good about a horse with experience on the track, the commotion at the showgrounds shouldn't faze her. Racetracks made bedlam look quiet.

I patted Esther's leg while I woolgathered and her hoof soaked. "Almost Esther," I said. "That's not a fair name for you, is it? It sounds as if you aren't as good as some other Esther, whoever that might be, and that can't be the case. You're a good girl. The best girl."

I'd inspected her lineage and there was no "Esther" of any variety in her bloodline. So, who was this other Esther to whom my Esther ought to be aspiring? If Esther knew, she wasn't telling.

Esther looked at me and pricked her ears and I managed a small smile, running my hand down her long, strong leg and thinking how lucky I had been to find her.

I sat in the quiet barn as the minutes ticked by and her foot finished soaking, and finally felt able to take a few calm breaths. I wondered if Cameron had gone back to his civil procedures book, and figured after the day's excitement it was unlikely he needed his energy drink anymore. On the other hand, if the past was any indication, he'd be up tonight studying long after I gave up and went to bed.

Finally, I lifted Esther's hoof from the bucket and dried it, put a poultice on the sole and wrapped it with vet wrap and a couple of pieces of duct tape. Then I finished the barn chores, cleaning stalls and bringing my other two boarder horses in for the night.

Songster, a pretty gray thoroughbred mare and AllBeCalm. I wasn't sure what AllBeCalm's breeding was, but he was far from calm. In fact, he was Catalpa's Very Bad Boy. He had horrible manners out in his paddock, and if he didn't stop kicking the stall wall, I was going to have to figure out some other strategy for having him inside. He'd have the barn torn down before I'd gotten through the first KHE event if he didn't break his leg first.

And, as I'd suspected, he wasn't happy that his evening meal was late. I managed to move him to the barn, but only after a certain amount of difficulty, and I was flushed and flustered by the time I got him inside.

I stopped at Donagin's stall and gave him another flake of hay. He came over so I could rub his face, and I was happy to see he had put a little bit of weight on his toe. I hoped he would be sound enough someday that he could be ridden, and perhaps someone could get him back in the show ring. I wondered if Joe's wife was a rider, or if she might sell Donagin once he recovered from his injury. He was a great horse. I was going to do my very best to help him.

"Tomorrow I've got to walk out and take a look at that jump," I told Donagin. "Make sure it's safe for other people to use."

I thought of the disturbed earth on the other side of the jump. Perhaps the horse had caught his foot on the top of the ramp and fallen? It seemed a bit odd, as Donagin was a seasoned jumper and Joe a skilled rider, but it bore looking into, if for no other reason than I could say I had done it.

Any good businesswoman needs to be able to say that.

Chapter Four

I didn't sleep well and awakened before my usual 6:00 AM, tiptoeing into the kitchen so as not to disturb Cameron. I clicked the coffeepot on and listened to its comforting burble, trying not to worry about what sorts of horrors today would bring.

Cameron joined me moments later, still in his pajamas. He looked down at me and yawned. "I couldn't sleep either. Wish I could go out with you and help check that jump, but I've got an exam in contracts and still have to mess with that civil procedures text. Most boring thing ever." Cameron ran his fingers through his sandy hair, making the front of it stick straight up. It was one of his most endearing habits.

I kissed him and pointed at his coffee cup sitting on the counter. "You concentrate on school. I can take care of the jump." He frowned, his hair so askew that I began to laugh, even though I didn't much feel like it. "I'll be fine. Just waiting for the coffee to perk and then I'm going to go get at it."

He nodded, yawned again, and turned back toward the bedroom, presumably to get dressed and start his day.

A few minutes later, I had donned stable clothes and gone out to the barn, clutching my coffee cup. I turned AllBeCalm and Songster out in their paddocks with grain and hay, filled water buckets, and then went to check on Donagin.

The big bay didn't look much different. He was still keeping his weight off his foot, but he was standing quietly. I debated whether or not to give him another dose of the reserpine Crystal had left, in case he got anxious. It was good that he and Esther would be inside together. It ought to help Donagin feel more comfortable. Horses being herd animals, they could get agitated being left alone in a barn.

I decided to give him a half dose of the sedative, then went on to feed Harry, Hermione and Ron, my three barn cats, their morning fare. I still had stalls to clean and the outside paddocks to go over, but it was so restful in the barn that I just didn't want to get started. I stood watching Harry, who was the glutton of the group, clean up all the food Ron had left behind, poured Hermione, who was the shy one, a few more crunchies in the corner where no one else could bother her, and bent to stroke Harry's broad back.

They were littermates I'd picked up from the Humane Society, and they couldn't have been more different. Harry, a brown tabby, was big and assertive; his sister, Hermione, was gray and white, and very timid; and Ron, the orange tabby, was somewhere in between. They kept the mice at bay in my barn and gave me some quiet moments sitting with them on the tack room floor, and I loved them all.

I knew I was procrastinating. I needed to get out to the woods and check the ramp jump, but I feared I'd see Joe Beers' lifeless body in my mind. The thought of that made me feel a little queasy.

Sighing, I gave my three cats a final stroke and

then strode out to the side-by-side and fired it up. I threw a shovel, a rake, a hammer, a pair of pliers and some nails in the back, just in case, then motored down the lane. *Thank God for these utility vehicles*, I thought. The side-by-side had been a large investment, but for moving stuff around—for example, out to the cross-country jump course—it was invaluable.

It was a crisp morning, and the horses were feeling their oats out in the paddock. As I rolled past, I saw AllBeCalm kick up his heels in a spectacular buck, and I yelled, "Knock it off. Settle down!" Which, of course, AllBeCalm ignored.

"AllBeCalm, indeed," I muttered. "I'm changing your name to Mayhem." It would be a private nickname, but all the same, no horse deserved it more.

The horses' riders would be out later in the morning, I knew, to put them through their paces and practice for the show. AllBeCalm, a.k.a., Mayhem could use a good workout to help him blow off excess energy. I dreaded the thought of explaining what had happened to Joe and had the cowardly notion that perhaps if I stayed out on the cross-country course long enough, everyone might be gone by the time I got back.

I couldn't linger out here forever. I had things to manage back at the barn.

I wondered when Esther's abscess might open up and was still pondering that when I rounded the corner and drove up to the ramp where Joe Beers had fallen. I killed the motor on the side-by-side and went to inspect the jump.

I looked at it from all sides, climbed up on top and bounced on the sloped slats, then checked the approach. Everything appeared fine. It was the trail that was damaged.

I walked to the other side of the jump and looked around, furrowing my brow. What had caused Donagin to go down? It could have been something completely random, of course. Horses did random stuff all the time. They shied from leaves, spooked at air, whatever. But Donagin was such a steady, professional, unflappable horse that it was hard to believe. The ramp wasn't a tall jump. Donagin had jumped much, much higher, and from harder angles and—likely—going much faster.

It looked as if the horse had taken the jump cleanly and then fallen on the other side, throwing Joe and causing a fatal neck injury.

I shuddered, gazing at the torn earth. Whatever had happened, it seemed Donagin had gone down heavily and struggled to regain his feet, disturbing a large area of soil and making an uneven dip in the smooth trail.

I began to use the shovel to move clods of earth back into place, then raked the area smooth and tamped it all flat. It was a lot of effort, and I felt a trickle of sweat slide down the back of my neck, but I was determined to make the path safe to use.

Taking a few steps away, I cocked my head and inspected my work, decided the torn area still wasn't smooth enough, and I raked more earth into the dip. It was an oddly deep impression. I knew it hadn't been there before because I walked the trails several times a week to make sure everything was safe, and to ensure there was no deadfall or miscellaneous debris blown over the paths.

I'd been out the day before Joe's accident, and all had been well.

I frowned and stared again at the cavity. It was mostly flat now, and the trail smooth and even, but I didn't like that the soil was rather soft where I'd filled in the deep spots. I needed to put up a sign in the barn warning people not to use this trail for a few days. And I should bring the roller out behind the side-by-side to give the area a good packing down.

My phone rang, and I pulled it out of my pocket to answer, wiping a drip of sweat off the tip of my nose.

"Catalpa Farm. Anna Parnell."

"Hello, Anna," came a musical woman's voice with a lilting Southern accent. "My name is Valentina Hirsch. I've got horses competing in the Keystone event, and I hear through the grapevine you might have some openings."

My stomach gave an excited leap. Word was getting around. *I might be able to sell a couple more stalls before KHE gets underway*, I thought. That would be a good income stream for Catalpa.

"I do, indeed," I answered. "Twelve by twelve box stalls and individual paddock turnout. How many horses?"

"Three."

I clutched my phone. *Three* horses. It was great news. I only had two empty stalls ready to go right now. I'd have to boot poor Esther out, but I had a paddock with a lean-to she could use for shelter.

"I can do that," I said with a calmness I wasn't feeling.

I was already making a to do list. Make the stalls spic and span. Get another load of shavings, buy clean water buckets …

" … bring our own feed," the woman was saying, and I tuned back into the conversation.

"That'll be fine. I require a one-month deposit. Will that work?"

"Yes."

"All right, let me get your details. Hang on." I dug in my pocket for a pen or pencil or any sort of writing implement, found the remains of a felt tip that had only a miniscule amount of ink left in it, and rescued a scrap of paper from under the passenger seat in the side-by-side. I was maneuvering the paper around so I could write down the caller's name and contact information, and I had just opened my mouth to say *Go ahead* when the paper blew out of my hand and into the woods.

"I'm sorry," I muttered. "I'll be right with you." I muted the call so any miscellaneous cursing I might be inclined to utter wouldn't be audible to her and trudged into the trees.

There was the paper, stuck saucily against a sapling a good five feet into a rather dense stand of maples just beyond the jump.

I stomped over to it, snatched it up and turned to go back to the side-by-side, then stopped and looked over my shoulder. I cocked my head, trying to make sense of what I was looking at. Then my heart began to hammer against my ribs. Tied around the sapling was a length of rope.

Some of it was hidden beneath a layer of wet leaves and scrub, but I could see the end, knotted around the little tree, pulled so tightly that the bark had torn away in spots.

I am by no means a tree expert, yet the wounds in the bark looked new to me. I felt my hands trembling and I stood motionless in the quiet woods, becoming more alarmed by the second.

What would this be doing here? It was a new rope, not one that had been out in the elements for any length of time. And the leaves looked disturbed, as if someone had deliberately buried the loose end.

What if ... My mind took a sudden wild and horrifying leap. What if the rope had been stretched across the cross-country trail to the other side of the ramp. And what if Donagin had taken the jump, then tripped. What if he hadn't fallen from a spook or some chance event. Maybe he'd gone down and Joe had been thrown off. The horse's struggles could have caused the damage to the tree. What was more, what I was seeing wasn't just any rope. It looked like a lunge line, a long rope used to train and exercise horses. I could see the clip where the rope was knotted at the tree. Lunge lines are typically twenty-five to thirty-five feet long. This rope belonged to someone who had horses, and it was plenty long enough to reach across the trail.

What if someone had deliberately caused the terrible accident?

For a moment, it felt as if my blood had turned to molten lava. If some monster had tripped that lovely horse, they deserved ... Well, I wasn't sure what punishment was bad enough for a person who would deliberately cripple an animal and kill a man.

But if anyone had done that hideous, heinous, *evil* thing, would they have left the rope behind? I tried to pull myself together. I had to be mistaken. I had let my imagination run out of control. I reached toward the rope, planning to pull it out from where it was hidden under the leaves.

"Hello? Are you still there?"

I jumped at the sound of the voice, and then realized I'd left my caller on mute for what had to have been several minutes. I'd almost forgotten about her.

"I'm so sorry!" I exclaimed, unmuting the call and putting the phone back up to my ear. I backed away from the sapling and its awful rope as if it might jump out and grab me.

Suddenly the woods seemed ominous and threatening. I looked over my shoulder. Nothing was there except the side-by-side, idling patiently back by the jump.

"Please give me your contact information," I said, trying to sound calmer than I felt, which was far from calm. Thoughts—none of them good—were whirling through my head, and I had the sickening sensation that someone was watching me, although a quick glance around seemed to show that I was alone.

I hurried back to the side-by-side, stumbling through the foliage and scrambling to keep my balance. "I'll email you the lease agreement in an hour or two. My boarding prices are there, and if everything looks okay to you, we can move on to next steps." All I wanted to do was get out of these woods and back to the barn. I was struggling not to pant.

"I'm in a bit of a hurry," the woman said, sounding irritated. I didn't blame her. She'd been waiting on hold for quite a while. "The Gold and Platinum barns are full, can you imagine? I'd never put a horse in the Bronze. It's a dump! These horses need schooling, and decent stalls. It's very tiresome. I had planned to stable at the showgrounds. The KHE staff must have gone mad. And," she went on tersely, "I'm not putting my horses in the temporary stalls. I'm not sure who would want to take that risk."

I knew KHE named their arenas and their associated stabling facilities after precious metals, so these statements weren't as strange sounding to me as they might otherwise have been. I also knew everyone wanted to get into either the Gold or the Platinum barns, as they were closest to the practice arenas. There was nothing wrong with the Bronze barn, but it was farther away. She hadn't mentioned Silver. Maybe it wasn't up to her standards either.

"Well, I hope you'll find Catalpa Farm to be a good substitute. Once I have the signed agreement, I can bring you in anytime. Did you want to send someone to look things over?" I knew my voice sounded breathless, but what I had seen in the woods had me more than a little panicked. I had to decide what to do about my discovery. Was I right about my suspicions?

"There's no need. I know someone who has … who has been there. He recommended you." I wondered who that was. I hadn't shown anyone around in several weeks. Valentina's musical voice brought me back to the present. "My email address is vhirsch@hirschequine.com. Did you get all that? Do you need the spelling of my name?"

"No, I have it." I hoped I did. I was distracted and frightened and having a very hard time concentrating.

I wrote down her contact information as best I could with my half-working felt tip on my tiny slip of paper, repeated it back to her, and then scrambled onto the side-by-side for a hurried trip back to the barn.

Chapter Five

Cameron was pulling into the driveway, finished with his morning at school, just as I parked the side-by-side by the barn and jumped off.

"Cameron!" I yelled. He had climbed out of the car and was heading for the house, but he changed direction when he heard my call.

He jogged up to me. "What's going on?"

I took a deep breath. "Everything, it seems. Someone called and wants to bring in *three* horses. I've got to send her the agreement and get everything ready, but that's not the least of it." I told him about fixing up the ramp jump and about my find in the woods, trying to make it sound as reasonable as possible. Unfortunately, the more I thought about it, the more I wondered if I'd been imagining things. Maybe the rope *had* been there all along. The trees were dense, and it would be impossible to see from the trail. Maybe I should have examined it more closely. After all ... what was I suggesting? That someone at Catalpa had committed murder?

"Wait, Annie." Cameron scrubbed at his hair and then put a hand on my shoulder. "What you're saying is that you think someone went out to the jump and waited for Joe to come along on Donagin, deliberately tripped him, and then ran away? How would they know he was out there? And which way he'd be going?"

"Um." I gave my non-horsey husband a careful look. "It's a ramp jump, so he had to approach it from the direction he did. It starts low and slants upward."

"But," Cameron's hair was getting a workout. "Who knew he was out there? And why wouldn't they take the rope away?"

"You're right! You're right!" I muttered. "But Cameron, I've had this feeling all along that something didn't make sense. I thought I was imagining things, but now I don't know what to do. I'm wondering if I should call the police."

Cameron looked startled. "Call the police? You sound pretty sure of this."

I sighed. "I'm not sure of anything. It's just weird. The rope was tied around a tree, but a lot of it was underneath the fallen leaves in the woods. As if it was deliberately hidden. Except ..." I hesitated. "I didn't pull it out to see if it would stretch to the other side of the jump. There are certainly plenty of trees over there to tie it to, and it is probably long enough. It was tied about eighteen inches off the ground. High enough to trip a horse." I felt another hot flush of anger. "I can see it happening. Donagin cleared the jump and started away at a gallop, hit the rope and down he went. In fact," my voice went up a couple of decibels. "The ground was all torn up there. Donagin fell and struggled up. Maybe he was tangled in the rope. Crystal thought he might have contact burns on his front legs. Maybe—"

Cameron held up a hand. "I think we should go back out and take a closer look."

"Oh ugh! I don't want to," I wailed. "I hate it out there. Plus, I've got to mail off the agreement to the woman who wants to stable the three horses, and Esther's foot needs soaking, and I've got to tend to Donagin and get those stalls ready, and—just ugh!" I was tempted to give my own hair a yank. I was beginning to see why Cameron found it so therapeutic.

"You hate it out there?" Cameron echoed. "Why?"

"Because ... Because Joe was killed, and I really think ... Cameron, I think that someone set it up for him to have that accident. The other stuff I need to do is just distractions. The big problem is what happened out at the ramp jump. I hope it'll turn out I'm mistaken, and it was an accident, but I don't think I am. And if I'm not mistaken, we shouldn't touch anything, you know? I already filled in the whole area where Donagin fell, so if there is anything to be seen there, it's long gone."

Cameron nodded, his face grim. "If you're that convinced, we need to get some help. Let's call the police."

"I think that's right," I said. "Oh dear, I hope that's right!"

"Don't doubt yourself," Cameron said firmly. "You saw what you saw."

We went into the house and I made the call, trying to explain calmly what had happened and what my suspicions were, and why. Cameron stood close by, his hand on my shoulder. I clicked to hang up the phone. "They're sending someone out."

I sat down in one of our kitchen chairs with a thump. "Oh Cameron, I just *hate* this, and truthfully, I'm a little scared. What if I'm wrong? And what if I'm *not* wrong?"

"If you're wrong, you're wrong, and it really was a horrible accident. But it sounds as if something happened out there. I don't blame you for being scared. The idea of a killer being loose isn't very comforting."

I shivered. "While we're waiting, I'm going to email that boarding agreement. Then, somehow I've got to get the chores done and the horses tended to. And I've got to get three more stalls ready for the new horses."

"Can I help?"

"Don't you have studying?"

"Well, yes. Some."

"Then you do that, and I'll do the stable work. That was the deal when we got this place, right? I'll get it done. Don't mind my complaining. I'm just upset."

"Yeah, but no one was supposed to get murdered," Cameron said darkly. "When the police arrive, I'll at least come with you to the spot where you found the rope."

"I appreciate it," I said.

The police officer who responded, Martina Lopez, never once made me feel as if I was wasting anyone's time. She took careful notes on what I had seen, then asked to be taken to the site. I drove her in the side-by-side out to the ramp jump, with Cameron squashed into the cargo area in the back. I tried to go carefully, but I couldn't help jouncing him, and he had a pained look when I glanced over my shoulder to see how he was doing.

"Please stop short of the site," Officer Lopez instructed, so I motored up to about fifty feet from the area and idled to a stop. Officer Lopez climbed out, and Cameron and I followed, Cameron rather stiffly.

"There's where it happened," I said, pointing toward the jump. "They found him just on the other side. The EMTs seemed to think it was a terrible accident when they came, and I didn't suspect anything different until I came out here today. I wanted to repair the damage to the trail so no one else took a fall. The path was very badly torn up before I filled it in. I assume the horse skidded or struggled ..."

Officer Lopez nodded, writing more notes. She took a couple of phone photos of the jump, the trail, and the surrounding area. "And where did you find the rope?"

I led her into the woods alongside the trail and toward the sapling, Cameron following closely behind. "I didn't touch it," I said over my shoulder. "You can see where it's tied around the tree. It's as if someone hid the rest of it under the leaves. I don't know if the rope is long enough to reach across the trail or not. It's right there." I stopped well away from the spot and gestured.

"Let me look," said Officer Lopez. "You two wait here, all right? I'm glad you didn't handle it."

She approached the tree, took photos of it, the rope, and the view from the tree to the jump. Then she bent to look at the ground where I'd thought the rest of the rope might be concealed, and she took several more phone pictures. I exchanged glances with Cameron, who looked grim.

"The bark on the tree is pretty damaged," Cameron pointed out, and Officer Lopez looked back at us.

"Yes, it does appear as if a lot of force was applied to this. I'm not going to disturb anything right now. I'm going to go look on the other side of the trail."

Officer Lopez made her way back through the woods, motioning to us to stay where we were. She walked across the path, glancing around and taking more photos. Then she stopped and examined another tree.

Even from a distance, I could tell that tree was older, but that there were faint marks on the bark. It seemed the rope had been tied on the other side of the bridle path, and the wounds didn't show as much as they had on the younger tree. There was no sign of a rope. If what I thought happened had really happened, the rope was still tied to the sapling. I felt a chill run up my arms. Cameron sensed my disquiet and clasped one of my cold hands in his.

Officer Lopez took more photos while Cameron and I returned to the side-by-side.

"Hey, what's going on?" The voice nearly made me jump out of my skin.

A slender man with white-blonde hair was standing in the low brush just beyond the ramp jump, but on the KHE side of the fence. He was wearing buff riding breeches and low paddock boots and had spectacular blue eyes. Officer Lopez walked out of the trees and approached him. "Who are you?" she said.

"J. D. Williams," the man said. "I'm over at the KHE for the show. Heard there was stabling nearby with a good cross-country course for schooling. What's going on?" he asked again.

"Did you walk from the showgrounds?" Officer Lopez asked.

"Well, yes. It isn't far. People are talking about this place, and I wanted to check it out. Is this where the accident—"

Officer Lopez cut him off. "There's an investigation underway here. You can talk to these people about making an appointment later." She gestured at Cameron and me over her shoulder.

I edged over to J. D. Williams. "I'm Anna Parnell. If you want to discuss stabling at Catalpa, drive out of the showgrounds and make a left. The entrance to this stable is on the lefthand side, about a mile down. You can't miss it. There's a sign that says Catalpa Farm."

"Easier to just walk through the trails," J. D. grinned and pointed, and I looked over at Officer Lopez. What was this man grinning about? He'd heard about Joe's death, and now he was interrupting a police function? Perhaps he was just a gawker, but his whole demeanor seemed inappropriate.

"Please be on your way," Officer Lopez repeated, more sternly this time. "Go to the stable entrance."

I started to hand him a business card, but I never, *ever* have one when I need it. I looked at him and shrugged, holding out open hands. "It's not hard to find at all," I said lamely.

He grinned again. "I'll drive over later."

Officer Lopez shot him a glance and didn't answer. He turned on his heel and began to walk back toward the KHE showgrounds with an easy stride, the sun glinting off his bright hair. Once he was out of earshot, she asked, "Do people often come through your property to speak to you?"

"I've never had it happen so far, but we just opened," I answered truthfully, "and I wouldn't have any way of knowing how many people might be wandering around back here. This is the first show at the KHE since we moved in. There's a fence at our property line, so I figured … well, I figured people at the show would stay on the other side."

Don't tell me I'm going to have to invest in some sort of a new obstacle, I thought grumpily. *Maybe hanging radioactive symbols on the fenceposts would help. I better at least put No Trespassing signs up.*

Officer Lopez nodded and went back into the

woods, donning a pair of gloves. I gave Cameron a swift look.

I had reached a disconcerting realization.

The woven wire fence between Catalpa and the KHE showgrounds was easy to climb. People attracted to the property could come in anytime they wished. It couldn't be done on horseback, so I didn't have to worry about unauthorized riders on the jump course, but still.

Being accessible was a good thing if it drew people to consider Catalpa as a place to keep their horses during the KHE shows. It was a bad thing if people did bad things when they walked onto the farm, like commit murder.

And it appeared pretty much anyone could have.

Chapter Six

"I need to ask some questions. Is there a place we can sit down for a few minutes?" Officer Lopez asked once we had driven the side-by-side back to where her cruiser was parked in the Catalpa lot. "I want to get some information from you."

I tried not to gulp. "We can go in the house," I offered. "Could I offer you a cup of coffee?"

"No, thank you. This won't take long, but I need to fill in some details."

I looked at Cameron. "Is it okay if my husband listens in?"

"Yes, that's all right." Officer Lopez paused to talk in a low voice on her radio, while I parked the side-by-side in its spot under the barn overhang. Then she followed Cameron and me into the house.

I gestured toward the dining room table and we sat down, Officer Lopez on one side and Cameron and I on the other. I felt Cameron pat my knee and I covered his hand with mine. I had the sudden awful realization that if the police decided there was foul play, I could very well be a suspect. But why would I kill Joe Beers? Why would anyone?

I began to feel rather sick.

"I've radioed for the crime lab team," Officer Lopez said. "They'll remove the rope, put tape around the site, and collect any evidence they can uncover. The area will be closed off for a while. You need to stay away from there and keep others away as well."

"Is there a chance it really was an accident?" I asked. "And all this is for nothing?" I paused. "I suppose if I'd been smart, I would have pulled the rope out of the leaves and checked it for horsehair. I didn't do that." Officer Lopez glanced at me. "It was better that I didn't, isn't it?" I asked.

She didn't comment and I exchanged looks with Cameron. In that moment, I was certain my pretty farm with the cross-country jump course I had put in so lovingly, was a crime scene.

"I'll put a sign up in the barn warning people away," I said miserably, "and I'll also call the people who have horses here."

Officer Lopez nodded. "I'll be getting in touch with all of them, too. Let's talk about what happened, okay?" She took out a notebook. "Start with who else is here at the stable besides you and your husband."

"Well, I board horses …" I began.

"Board?" she asked.

"Yes. As you just saw, the Keystone Horse Exhibition grounds are right next door to this farm, and the KHE shares a boundary with this property. I rent stalls to people who are going to the shows there." I watched as Officer Lopez made notes. "We just opened this year," I said. "The show that is coming up soon is the Special, and it's a big deal."

"Meaning?" Officer Lopez looked up at me.

"Um," I hesitated. "Meaning, I guess, that it's the biggest event of the year at KHE, and a lot of very valuable horses and professionals show there."

"And why wouldn't they stay at the exhibition?"

"Because here is quieter, and because sometimes they can't get the barn they want. I probably have three more horses coming in soon that will be showing at KHE. Their owner wanted a certain barn and couldn't get it."

"Okay, go on. And how many people are renting from you?"

"Well, just two right now. I had three boarder horses, but then Joe ..." My voice trailed off.

I gave Officer Lopez the names of the other two people with horses boarded at Catalpa. Jason Barlowe, who owned AllBeCalm, and Marcy Katz, who rode Songster.

Officer Lopez wrote down their names, then gestured at her notes. "Go on. Continue with the story. What happened the day of the incident?"

I shrugged. "I already told you a lot of it."

"Tell me again."

I felt a chill run up my arms. "Well, yesterday Joe Beers's horse came back to the barn riderless, and I went out looking for Joe. I found him out on the cross-country course—I mean the trails and jumps that go through the woods and fields."

"Who else was here when this happened?"

"No one. I was at the farm all by myself. Even Cameron was out. He went to run a couple of errands."

"And Mr. Beers was riding on the trails alone?"

"Yes. He'd already done his schooling for the show, and he liked to ride the cross-country for fun. There isn't a cross-country competition at the Special, but I built the course out there for some other smaller shows, and because riders enjoy getting away from the arenas sometimes." I paused awkwardly, but Officer Lopez didn't comment, so I went on. "The day after it happened—that is, today—I went to make sure the trail and the jump were all right for other people to use—"

"Who else would use them?"

"I'm not sure," I said slowly. "Jason Barlowe doesn't. Maybe Marcy? Or someone else I bring in later? I don't know? Anyone who boards here. Not outsiders."

"And who might you be bringing in?"

"So far, I only have the one person I already mentioned, and she's tentative. She needs to sign the boarding agreement still. The competition goes on for multiple weeks, so I imagine—I hope—I'll get some more boarders soon. Other horses competing in the Special, maybe. But after the Special, there's a dressage show ... dressage is where people ride movements to patterns," I hurriedly explained, "and don't jump. Then after the dressage show, there are other competitions all summer long."

"Okay. I understand," Officer Lopez turned a page in her notebook. "Go on."

"I didn't like how the trail was all torn up after the accident and I wondered if the jump had been damaged, so I went out to look."

"And was it damaged?"

"The jump was fine, but the trail was bad. I filled in all the holes and raked it smooth. I planned to go out with a roller, but that was before I found the rope. I'm sorry I did that—filled in all the holes, that is. I didn't know I shouldn't. I just wanted to make sure my place was nice. And safe," I added. I forced my voice not to waver. I was getting more upset by the minute.

"And how did you find the rope?"

I explained about the call from Valentina, and

how my paper had blown away. "I walked into the woods and up to the tree," I said, "but I didn't touch anything. I was so shocked when I saw it. I just stood there."

"And why did it alarm you?"

I hesitated again and felt Cameron's fingers tighten on my knee. Was I saying the right thing? Was I a suspect in Joe's death?

I took a deep breath. "First of all, there was no reason for a rope to be there, on my property. I could tell it hadn't been there for very long because it wasn't dirty or wet or anything. And I sort of put two and two together. Joe was an expert rider, and his horse is just—well, his horse just doesn't make mistakes over jumps. Especially not over a jump like that one. Any horse could shy or bolt or something, I know, but then the combination of the rope and how torn up the area was. And the horse is injured. I had the vet see to him the day Joe fell. He's all cut up, and he's got a pretty bad tendon injury. He went down really hard. The vet also mentioned the wounds on the horse's front legs. She said they could be burns. I looked at the rope and where it was, and somehow I just knew. Or at least suspected. I think Joe's horse has rope burns on his legs," I finished awkwardly.

There was a long silence while Officer Lopez wrote.

"And did you touch anything in the woods?" she asked.

I hesitated. "I know I touched the sapling, because that's where my paper was. I probably touched some of the other trees, too," I said. "I was sort of climbing around in there." I shrugged. "I'm not sure. I don't remember. Except I'm positive I didn't touch the rope."

Officer Lopez nodded. "What else?"

"Nothing that I can think of," I said. "I finished the call and then ran for the side-by-side and came up to the house. I told my husband what I'd seen, and then we phoned you."

"You said someone contacted you about boarding. Did you tell the caller what you'd found?"

"No, I didn't. I just wrote down her name and email address and then came home."

Officer Lopez looked at Cameron. "Do you have anything to add?"

He shook his head. "I wasn't here when the accident occurred. I went out there for the first time when you came today. Annie told me what happened, though, and it's just as she explained."

"Who else have you told?"

I grimaced. "Everyone knows about Joe's death. Everyone here, and I'm sure just about everyone over at the showgrounds by now, but I haven't talked to anyone about the rope. I just found it, and I wouldn't have known what to say anyway."

"Let's keep it that way, shall we? Don't share the details until we know more."

"Yes, of course. Wait, I also talked to the vet—Crystal Ellis. The one who treated the horse. She's a good friend of mine, too. But that was yesterday. Not today after ... after I came back from checking the jump."

"Do you have her contact info?"

I nodded, looked it up on my phone and read off the information.

"I'll also need contact information for ..." Officer Lopez looked down at her notes. "Ms. Katz and Mr. Barlowe."

"I'll get that for you."

"Thank you. What about the gentleman who

called to us over the fence?"

I shrugged and scowled as I felt a tickle of irritation. "I've never met him. I don't know what he was doing there. I've got to think what to do about people wandering over from the showgrounds. I can't have them doing that."

"I wouldn't want that, either, if I were you. Is there anything else you can remember or that you haven't told me?"

I shook my head. "Not right now. If I remember something, I'll call you right away."

Officer Lopez stood. "Thank you. The crime lab team should be here in a few minutes."

Cameron and I walked her to the door and stood watching as she strode to her cruiser, spoke into her radio, and then leaned against the door, scanning her notes.

My husband put his arm across my shoulders, and I felt tears well up in my eyes. "I have an awful feeling she thinks I'm involved somehow," I said.

"Well, you aren't," he answered. "She has to ask these questions, but it only means she's trying to get to the bottom of what happened. It's all part of the process. Don't worry."

"It's hard not to. Do you think she believes someone killed Joe?"

"It sure seems as if she does," Cameron replied. "I don't think she would have called the crime lab techs out if she didn't."

"Poor Crystal. I feel as if I painted a target on her," I said.

"You didn't paint a target on her," Cameron assured me. "There's no reason for them to suspect Crystal had anything to do with Joe's death. Officer Lopez will probably ask about Donagin's injuries and if they're consistent with him being tripped. That's my guess."

"Okay," I said haltingly, and then looked up at Cameron.

"Oh, Cameron," I said. "How could this have happened? It's just so hard to believe. Someone *killed* him? Joe Beers? Who would do that?"

"They'll find out," Cameron said. "They'll figure out who did it and also why."

Just then another vehicle rolled into the parking lot and a man and a woman wearing police vests climbed out.

I sighed. "Here we go," I said, and went out to meet them.

Chapter Seven

That evening, I sat at my desk, papers strewn across my laptop and onto the floor, several file folders open, and my head in my hands.

Valentina Hirsch's transport company was arriving the next day from Kentucky with her three horses. She'd returned the agreements right away and sent me her deposit for the coming month, a hefty sum that I hoped would help balance the Catalpa books for the short run. I should be happy, but instead I was asking myself for the fiftieth time if I'd gone crazy to think I could run this place.

The crime scene people had been out at the ramp jump for over three hours that afternoon. I'd tried to stay focused on what I needed to do at the barn, but I kept looking down the lane for them to return and wondering what they had found. Had they uncovered any evidence that might explain Joe's mishap? Whom would it implicate? Or would no one be implicated? Perhaps it really had been a freak accident.

My hopes had been dashed when the lead for the team informed me that they'd put up crime tape all around the ramp jump site, and that everyone at Catalpa needed to stay strictly away until the police had completed their investigation.

Disheartened, I'd gone back to work, prepping the three stalls for the Hirsch horses, doing chores, tending to Esther's foot and settling her in the run-in paddock. Then I mucked out stalls, met Crystal for the check on Donagin, repaired a paddock rail AllBeCalm had destroyed, and had a lengthy and altogether unpleasant discussion with AllBeCalm's owner, Jason Barlowe. I was still smarting from that.

AllBeCalm had a cut on one of his forelegs, one that I hadn't seen when I turned him out, but I wasn't feeling sympathetic—the horse had bitten me when I tried to get his halter on. In fact, I was feeling decidedly irritable and defensive. The cut was miniscule, and Jason might not have noticed it at all, had there not been a small smear of blood on AllBeCalm's white stocking. And the injury was probably not caused by anything I'd done. Likely AllBeCalm had inflicted it on himself during his shenanigans in the paddock, which were legion. Cameron had commented on it the previous evening.

"You sure that bay in the second paddock isn't actually a rodeo bucking horse? He sure acts like one." I had no answer.

Jason informed me that he held me responsible for the cut having happened, for not noticing it, for not informing him that AllBeCalm had injured himself, and for running a "slack shop." Then he told me that if there had been decent stalls open at KHE—I presumed that meant even in the Bronze barn—he'd be gone in a second. All of his diatribe was delivered in the clipped British accent that sounded so lovely when uttered by others, but coming from Jason, it was like being stabbed with a dagger.

Jason was a big man, muscular and athletic, with a narrow austere face and dark, wavy hair that he pulled back in a ponytail. He would have been a good-looking man if I had ever, *ever* seen him smile, but he seemed opposed to it. Everything he said appeared designed to wound or to insult, and it definitely worked.

I apologized, promised to keep a close eye on Mayhem, asked if Jason would like to have the veterinarian take a look at his horse, and tried not to sigh when he turned on his heel and stalked away without answering.

What I didn't discuss with Jason was that AllBeCalm was still kicking his stall wall. After the drubbing he'd given me, I didn't dare bring it up.

And it was my problem, after all. I had to figure out something. Investing in padding wasn't my first choice, but ... perhaps I should have at least one padded stall standing by for the future anyway. AllBeCalm wasn't the only horse in the world who entertained himself by kicking the walls.

Cameron set his hand on my shoulder. "What'cha doing?"

I pulled myself back from my spinning thoughts. "Driving myself crazy," I answered. "Trying to do bookkeeping, trying not to think evil thoughts about AllBeCalm and Jason Barlowe, trying to find a stapler, and Crystal thinks I need a logo. What do you think of this drawing? Or this?"

"AllBeCalm. Is that the rodeo horse?"

"That's the one. He's apparently very talented in the show ring, but he takes a special rider. It surprises me Jason has the patience for him." I shrugged.

"Jason's his trainer?"

"And owner," I said. "He doesn't have a trainer that I know of. I think Jason would drive a trainer nuts, quite frankly. He's got a rather abrupt—if not downright mean—personality. Seems as if he's the wrong rider for a sensitive horse."

"Sensitive?" Cameron echoed.

I smiled grimly. "Or maybe just badly-behaved." I wiggled the two papers I was holding in my hands. "Do you like either of these logos?"

"Hmm." Cameron looked at one drawing and then at the other. "It's clever how you worked the catalpa leaves into it. But honey, you should probably get a professional to design something for you."

"They're just mock-ups," I protested. "And the leaves are the basis for the whole thing. But if you think they're awful, then ..." I tossed the papers down and scowled. "Maybe I don't need a logo."

"I think a logo'd be nice. And your drawings aren't awful." Cameron sat down next to me and retrieved my stapler from under a pile of envelopes. "What's really bothering you? Not the logo, surely."

I sniffed. "Aside from Joe Beers?"

Cameron didn't answer, but he covered one of my hands with his.

I slumped in my chair. "Well, the KHE is coming up soon, and I don't have a full barn. Crystal has been spreading the word over at the showgrounds, and she thinks it would be helpful to have a flyer or brochure or something, *ergo*, a logo. But at this point, maybe everyone thinks it's bad luck over here. Plus, the back of the cross-country jump course is closed. There's warning tape up all around the ramp jump. Crime scene techs were back there for several hours doing who-knows-what. Gathering evidence, I presume. They said not to go past the tape, which is fine, but unless I figure out where to put another trail, a lot of the cross-country path isn't usable. I have the feeling that's not going to make people around here happy."

"But there's no cross-country competition at the Special, right?" Cameron pointed out.

"No, but still." I crossed my arms. "It's amazing to me that neither of the people with horses here is asking questions about what happened to Joe. I'm sure the police have been in touch with them," I went on. "Marcy was here today—she's the one with that gray mare, Songster—and she didn't say anything. Neither did Jason, although he was too busy bawling me out to ask any questions. I shudder to think what Valentina Hirsch and her trainer are going to think. They're the ones that are arriving tomorrow. And I have this awful feeling that they'll just suddenly pull out."

"Courage," Cameron said. "You told them all what happened. Now there's not much more to ask you. They're probably talking like mad to each other. I think these are growing pains, and it'll work out."

"Maybe. And maybe it'll work out when we're in the poorhouse. I don't think growing pains includes people getting killed."

"Very true. But we won't go into the poorhouse. How many horses have you got right now?"

"Seven. Esther, who isn't a paying customer, obviously, Donagin, Songster, and AllBeCalm. Then the three coming in tomorrow."

"And isn't the show fourteen weeks long?"

"Well, yes.

"So, you've got fourteen weeks to recruit some more horses. They'll cycle in and out, right? Maybe it's better that you have turnover and not all of them all at once. If you have ten here, and seven there, then ..."

"I suppose you're right," I said, reluctantly. I sat up straight in my chair. "I just get so panicked sometimes.

The hunter competition is first; jumpers after that. Then the dressage show starts once the jumpers have cleared out and the Special is over. Crystal told me there are a lot of complaints about the Bronze barn. Maybe the dressage people won't like it either."

"See," said Cameron.

"I'd like twenty horses through here for the run of the Special," I said. "But I've got stalls to get ready in case a bunch come at once."

"Better get going," Cameron grinned, and I mock-punched him in the arm. "And speaking of, I better get going on civil procedures. I still have half the text to finish." He made a face, stood and patted the top of my head. "By the way, I like the design on the left best."

He went into his study and closed the door quietly behind him while I stared down at the sketches I'd done. The catalpas were one of the things that had drawn me to this property. Two of the sprawling trees, with their iconic heart-shaped leaves and long seed pods, arched over the entrance to the farm and welcomed visitors into their cool, green shade.

What's really bothering you? Cameron had asked.

What was really bothering me was the death of Joe Beers. I'd liked and respected Joe, and now he was dead.

And what was also bothering me was the thought that the enormous financial gamble we'd taken as a couple wouldn't pan out. Not because of my care of the horses. Not because of the quality of the facilities.

But because at Catalpa Farm, people got killed.

Chapter Eight

I woke up the next morning with a mysterious spurt of energy, took a deep breath and ordered pads for Mayhem's stall while trying to ignore the balance on our credit card. Then I did morning chores, turned horses out in their paddocks, made sure the stalls were all set for the Hirsch horses, and checked on Donagin.

I could tell he was still very lame, but as I led him out of his stall to clean it, his patient head bobbing at my shoulder, I thought maybe he didn't seem quite so hesitant to step on his injured foot.

I patted him on the neck. "You're a class act, pretty guy," I murmured as I led him into a different stall to have his grain and his meds.

I'd send Crystal an update later.

I was glad to see that Esther seemed none the worse for wear for her change in venue. She whickered at me from the shed and walked happily over for her morning hay and grain rations. I soaked and wrapped her foot, explaining to her that it was time she put some effort into getting that abscess to break through. If nothing happened by tomorrow maybe Crystal could hollow it out. It needed to drain before it could heal.

The pads for Mayhem's stall would be arriving in

the afternoon—at an extra charge for express delivery, of course—and Valentina's horses were scheduled to roll in just before noon. I had a few minutes and I wanted to call Elsa Kurchner.

I went into my barn office, which adjoined the tack room, and closed the door. Jason was out riding, but Marcy Katz, Songster's trainer, would be arriving any minute and I didn't want to be interrupted.

Elsa answered on the second ring, and I could tell she'd been crying, as she sounded very congested and a bit hoarse.

"Hey, Elsa," I greeted her. "Anna Parnell here. I wanted to update you on Donagin."

"Oh, hi, Annie," Elsa sniffed. "I almost didn't answer. I'll add you to my contacts. I should have done that already, but ..."

"I understand," I answered. "Is this a good time? I can talk to you later."

"No, I want to hear how Donagin is doing. I'm just standing by here at home, waiting until they release Joe's b-body. They're flying him home, you know."

"I'm so sorry." I hesitated. "Well, as far as Donagin's concerned, I think he's making good progress. He is on total stall rest for the next couple of days, but I can already tell he's a little less sore. The vet says if he stays quiet, I can start hand-walking him, maybe day after tomorrow or something. And in a couple of weeks he can be walked under saddle. Only walking, but it's a baby step up."

"That's wonderful, thank you."

"Do you have someone to ride him? I can do it, but maybe you have someone else in mind?"

"Oh, would you do it?" she asked. Her voice wavered and there was a long pause on the other end of

53

the line. It took a full minute before she was back, sounding more upset than ever. "I'll pay you, of course."

I opened my mouth to say, *Let's don't worry about that*, thought of Catalpa's credit card bill, and opted for, "I'm happy to help." I'd turned down her offer to pay before, but it wasn't practical to continue indefinitely. "He's just a wonderful horse, Elsa. So calm and easy to handle."

"I'm glad." Elsa sniffed. "I'll be a lot happier when Joe's body arrives home here in Miami. They're doing an autopsy, and then I can make plans for the memorial." Now she was openly sobbing. "They're saying … They're saying …"

"I know." How horrible to be told your husband was the victim not just of a sport he'd loved, but of foul play. I waited while she got her voice under control again. "If there's anything I can do, let me know."

"I will. I'm going through Joe's papers now. It's very strange and upsetting. Some of what I found made me wonder how well I knew Joe."

I pulled my phone away and stared at the display, disconcerted by this bit of confidence. This was only the second time I'd ever talked to Elsa. I wondered why she was choosing to disclose this to me. I was practically a stranger.

But Elsa wasn't done. "I told you we haven't been married very long," she went on, and I put the phone back to my ear. "But we loved each other, we really did."

"Of course," I murmured, at a loss for what to say.

"I'm trying to find documents and papers that I need among his things, but I'm having a terrible time. His desk is just an awful tangle …" her voice trailed off, and I waited, but perhaps she'd decided not to continue after all, because she cleared her throat and said, "Would you be willing to clean out Joe's tack cabinet and ship the things to me?"

"Of course," I said again. "He's got a trunk here, but also a locker with a padlock. If you email me permission, I'll cut the padlock off the locker and send everything to you."

"That's so helpful," Elsa said. "Keep anything you need for Donagin, but please ship anything that seems ... um ... personal, or that you don't want."

"I'll do that," I assured her.

That I don't want, echoed in my mind. Those words sounded so ... so throwaway. The equipment Joe owned was worth a small fortune. I probably could buy three saddles for what he'd paid for his. What if something happened to his tack while it was in my barn? Yet, Joe's saddle would've been adjusted to fit Donagin. I'd keep it till Donagin went back to Florida. And his bridle and bit, too. I'd just be super careful. Everything else could go.

I gave Elsa my email address and we signed off.

Valentina's horses arrived right on schedule, three shining beauties that walked quietly and obediently into their clean stalls—none of them another Mayhem. I helped unload the hay and grain Valentina had shipped with them, set up a tack locker, and asked when the trainer might arrive.

The van driver scratched his head. "She was right behind me when we made the turn, but maybe she pulled off for something." Just then a white BMW convertible swung into the driveway and rolled to a stop in the Catalpa parking lot. A tall, red-haired woman stepped out.

She walked up to me, her hand out. "Jessica Page," she said. "I'm Ms. Hirsch's trainer."

Ms. Hirsch, I thought. *And that car!* But I pretended to take it all in stride as I led Jessica to the barn, in the back of my mind wondering if I'd called Valentina Hirsch by her first name in our phone conversation, and whether I should start by addressing her as Ms. Hirsch. And what about Jessica Page? Ms. Page?

Growing pains, Cameron would've said if he hadn't been off at school. I needed to get acclimated to the very high-end world of professional horse showing.

Jessica introduced me to the three horses. Goldrush, a solid bay mare like my Esther; Paladin, a chestnut gelding with four white socks; and MidnightInVerona, a black mare with a narrow stripe down her face. I fell in love with Midnight immediately. She was not only gorgeous, but she had sweet, kind eyes and the endearing habit of running over to say hello to anyone who happened by her stall.

To my relief, Jessica pronounced herself delighted with the facilities, and began to move tack and supplies into the locker I'd assigned to the Hirsch crew.

I decided to take the plunge. "Does Valentina Hirsch wish to be called Ms. Hirsch or Valentina? I wasn't sure."

Jessica laughed. "Oh, you can call her Valentina. I just called her Ms. Hirsch in front of the van driver."

I gave Jessica a quizzical look but decided to drop it. I could always ask Valentina what she preferred. I resolved to look up Jessica Page on the Internet when I was back in the house. I had heard her name before, I was sure of it. I'd probably seen her in one of the show mags I scattered around the tack room. I had the feeling she was big in the horse show crowd.

Marcy Katz, Songster's trainer, arrived a few minutes later and she and Jessica wandered off, chatting amiably, clearly acquainted from the show circuit.

Neither Jason Marlowe nor Marcy said anything to me about the closed section of the cross-country course, which I still thought was rather odd. It seemed as if they had to be curious. The horse community was sprawled over the entire world but was very close-knit. I knew by now the news of Joe's death would have spread far and wide, and once it was known that the crime team had been at Catalpa, it was hard to believe people wouldn't be looking with suspicion at me and at my beloved farm.

I set my jaw and walked on. *Please let this all be over soon!* I thought.

I checked the three Hirsch horses to make sure they were comfortable, helped the van driver negotiate the tight turn around the circle drive, and went up to the house to check my email.

Elsa hadn't wasted any time. Her permission to break into Joe's locker was waiting for me, so I gathered up a carton and a pair of bolt cutters and headed back down to the barn right away. I didn't know what was in Joe Beers' locker, but I wanted to get it sent off to Elsa as quickly as I could, along with any of his other equipment I didn't need for Donagin.

Marcy was saddling Songster for her training session when I walked into the barn, Jessica standing close by. Jessica rummaged in her pocket and pulled out a treat for Songster, which made me smile.

The two young women looked quizzically at the bolt cutters I was carrying. "Will you ride today?" I asked

Jessica to distract her from asking questions. "Should I put your three out in paddocks or leave them in?"

"I'll ride tomorrow," Jessica said airily, gesturing at the stalls. "You can turn them out." So, I moved to let the newcomer horses outside for a bit of air, pausing to give MidnightInVerona an extra pat as I unsnapped her lead rope and watched her trot to the back of her paddock. One of the advantages of having Catalpa was being able to see and handle some spectacular horseflesh. Donagin was one such, and now Midnight.

I watched for a moment longer, then, hefting my bolt cutters, I headed for the row of lockers in the tack room, grateful that Marcy and Jessica were elsewhere, and Jason hadn't arrived yet to ride AllBeCalm. I had some time to myself.

I bent to my task, bolt cutters at the ready and Harry winding around my feet. I realized I still needed to feed my three barn cats. Cat food, next on the agenda.

Then, to my annoyance, Jason Barlowe walked in, Mayhem's saddle over his arm. I must have missed seeing his car drive in. He stopped, startled, when he saw what I was doing. "Is that standard practice?" he asked, rather nastily, I thought.

I tried to ignore him. "Just getting Joe's things back to their rightful owner." I leaned on the bolt cutters and the padlock gave way with a snap.

The cats scattered, and I watched with amusement as Jason bent and stroked Hermione, who had hidden behind his leg. Harry and Ron, also deciding that flying bits of metal was above their pay grade, had transferred their attention to Jason as well.

"Anything of interest?" Jason asked, moving a little to one side as I pulled open the door. He peered over my shoulder.

"I haven't had the chance to look yet," I answered rather sharply and closed the door a little. *I haven't had the chance to look yet, and it's none of your business*, I thought, but didn't say.

I waited for a moment and Jason finally moved on, my three cats following. He stepped carefully around them and arranged his saddle on the rack assigned to him, bent and gave Harry a scratch on the head.

"They're hungry," I said. "Sorry."

Jason didn't answer, but strode out of the tack room, my cats hot on his heels. *Fine*, I thought sourly. *If that grouch is more interesting than having breakfast, go for it, you ridiculous cats.*

Since the tack room was empty again, I pulled down the bag of dry cat food, poured crunchies into my cats' bowls, put a few extra nuggets back where Hermione liked to hide, and returned to Joe's locker.

The locker mostly contained the sort of items you would expect. A couple of extra brushes, a pair of buff riding breeches, a rain slicker, a clean saddle pad, a silver flask—that one surprised me. I shook it and heard liquid slosh inside. Another thing I'd have to consider. Allow drinking on the premises, or no? That one should be a hard stop. No drinking in the stable.

There was a packet of papers on the shelf and I pulled that out, ready to drop them into the carton when something caught my eye. It was the name *Catalpa* scrawled on top of something that looked like a receipt.

Feeling slightly guilty, I glanced over my shoulder to be sure no one was watching and tugged it out. It was a ledger sheet of payments for something. Something expensive. The opening balance was $72,500. I ran my eyes down the sheet and realized with a start that it was the payment record for a horse, apparently bought from

Joe Beers. I turned the paper over, knowing I was snooping, but I couldn't help it.

It was a photocopy, something Joe was probably keeping for his records, although why put it in his locker? Then I saw the rest of the note that had caught my eye.

With a gulp, I realized that the horse in question was AllBeCalm. The buyer, Jason Barlowe; the seller, Joe Beers.

And it appeared Jason was behind on his payments for AllBeCalm. Seriously behind.

Handwritten on the top was a note.

Jason: I'll have at least one horse at Catalpa Farm for KNE. We need to talk when you arrive.
Joe

Chapter Nine

"But doesn't it seem a little odd," Cameron asked me, as we talked that evening, "that Jason Barlowe and Joe Beers both chose Catalpa as a place for their horses? You'd think they would avoid each other like the plague!"

We were sitting out on the deck in the gentle evening sunshine enjoying a glass of wine in what Cameron called our Discussion Zone. There were rules for the DZ. No phones to distract us. Everything had to be taken seriously and at least considered, and no arguments.

Cameron and I didn't argue too terribly often, but the occasional ruffled feathers did happen and—like all married couples—sometimes we had to work to reach a compromise. But we'd been married for seven years, and despite the old saw about the Seven Year Itch, we were content. We'd promised each other we'd let each other know if we weren't, but so far that hadn't happened. I didn't think it would.

I took a sip of my wine, swallowed, and said, "My guess? Joe was here to keep an eye on Jason, and on his horse, AllBeCalm that is. Jason was … maybe? … here because it's a little less expensive at Catalpa than at KHE. Maybe he was trying to save some money. He's really in debt to Joe. I wonder if they ever had their talk?"

Cameron shrugged.

"I had to buy kick pads today for Mayhem's stall," I went on. "Even if Jason hadn't chosen to bring his horse to Catalpa, the KHE wouldn't want him there."

"Mayhem," Cameron grinned. I smiled back and tipped my wine glass in a salute.

"Not very smart on their part," Cameron went on. "The KHE, I mean. To run out of choice stabling space. It's good for us, but I'd think this would be a major black eye for them. It's a huge event, and the riders that come in are going to be very particular."

"I'll say. The Bronze and Silver barns aren't exactly tumbledown, but the show that's about to begin, the Special, is the premiere event east of the Mississippi for this time of year. International competitors and the whole thing. The Wellington events in Florida will overtake it in the winter, but for right now if you've got a high-level horse, the KHE is the place to be. And people are going to be ultra-picky about accommodations."

Cameron swirled his wine in his glass and narrowed his eyes. "$72,500 is a lot for a horse."

I shrugged. "It's a lot, but not necessarily for a horse in this circuit."

Cameron rolled his eyes. "You could buy a nice chalet in the Rockies for that."

"No, you couldn't," I said, feeling a twinge of remorse. We'd spent buckets to buy Catalpa. Not enough for a chalet in the Rockies, but definitely for a good down payment on one. And if we had a chalet, Cameron could have followed his lifelong dream of skiing. He was a good skier, but he'd given it all up, and—

"Don't make that face," my husband said. "If we were living in a chalet, how could I be in law school?"

"Well, you prob'ly could somehow," I replied

grumpily, and Cameron laughed.

"You're making that face again."

I sighed. "I hope this works out, Cameron. I keep having all these doubts."

"It will work out. Absolutely. And I'm behind you all the way."

I reached over and slipped my hand into his. He squeezed my fingers. "I just wish all this with Joe Beers hadn't happened. I mean, murder? On our farm? And now I'm wondering how Jason Barlowe plays into it. Should I tell anyone that he owed all that money to Joe? The police?"

Cameron thought for a minute. "Well, just because Jason owed Joe money doesn't mean Jason would do anything to hurt Joe. Besides, if he owes the money, he'd still owe it after Joe died. The debt wouldn't just go away. He'd owe Joe's estate. To Eva, right?"

"Elsa," I corrected. "Yes, that's true. Unless Elsa doesn't know about it?"

"A $72,500 debt? If I were married to him, I'd be one righteously angry person if he didn't let me know about a transaction like that."

I didn't answer. Yes, I'd be righteously angry, too. But this was the world of expensive—really expensive—show horses, some of them costing more than the average person, like me, could comprehend. What *did* Elsa know? Was there a way to find out?

I scrunched up my face. "I'd like to ask Elsa, but I guess there's no need. When she gets the shipment of Joe's things, she'll see the ledger sheet, just like I did."

"True. Inquiring minds, but … very true." Cameron smirked.

"I'll head over to UPS and get the boxes sent off to Elsa tomorrow. What a challenge this has all been. And it's just my first KHE show."

"Many such journeys are possible ..." Cameron said in a spooky voice, echoing the time travel Gateway in my favorite vintage *Star Trek* episode.

"That's what I'm afraid of," I said. I stood up, gathering up Cameron's empty wine glass. "Well, onward and upward. I'm going to go check on the horses."

Cameron smiled. "Good deal. I'm going to ... guess."

"Read civil procedures?"

"Got it in one." He bent to kiss me and started toward his study while I put the wine glasses in the dishwasher.

Out in the barn, I checked on all my charges, made sure Esther was happy, and took a special pass by Mayhem's stall. While he was out in his paddock creating havoc that afternoon, I'd employed a drill and smooth-headed screws to fasten the new kick pads to the walls, and I was quite pleased with the result. I bought the tallest ones I could find—four feet high—and they lined the stall like protective armor. I couldn't help but think of an inmate in a padded cell. Mayhem was that type.

He was standing quietly, though, the most contrary animal on the planet. I was sure if I moved him to a different stall without kick pads he'd be letting loose with both hind legs. I scowled at him and walked on.

Midnight looked at me curiously as I strolled by, and I stopped to pat her on the neck, peeking into her feed bucket to be sure she'd finished up her dinner.

Tomorrow, I needed to call Crystal and talk to her about checking Esther's foot when she did Donagin's follow-up ultrasound. I'd give Elsa a call as well and confirm that Joe's belongings were on the way to her.

I stopped to close the tack room door that

someone had left open and had to shoo my trio of cats out into the main part of the barn, lest they be shut in all night. Harry and Ron scampered out immediately. Hermione was nowhere to be seen.

"Kitty kitty?" I called, but there was no sign of her.

Frowning, I walked back into the tack room and then I spied her, sound asleep behind Jason Barlow's saddle rack, curled up on a pad that I knew was Jason's by the *JB* inscribed on the quilted corner. I gently dislodged her, much to her annoyance, and she made her dignified way out to join her feline friends.

I gave the pad a shake. It wouldn't do to have Jason's saddle pad covered with cat hair. I didn't care to have another scolding from him when he showed up the next day. I debated whether I could wash it tonight without him knowing.

But then I saw another pad sitting folded on top of his saddle and I scanned the one I held in my hand. It was an old one, frayed in one corner, and not a piece of equipment Jason would likely be caught dead using.

The only explanation I could conjure was that Jason had put the pad down behind his saddle in a private corner for Hermione to use. I put it back where it came from and shook my head. I tried to imagine that haughty, arrogant man acting gently toward a timid cat, but my imagination balked.

I let myself out of the tack room, took one last look down each of the barn aisles, shut off the lights, and walked toward the house, shaking my head.

Maybe that was why I liked animals so much. Humans were just mystifying.

Chapter Ten

I woke up the next morning wondering about making a list of Catalpa horse boarders and their trainers or riders to hang on the barn bulletin board. I had my own list, of course, with emergency names and numbers, etc., but I was thinking of something a little nicer. Something to make the farm more social, although it seemed as if most of my renters already knew each other, probably through show circles.

But I was determined, so after morning chores and turnout, and my visit to UPS, I fired up my computer and printer and began a sign.

AllBeCalm – Jason Barlowe
Almost Esther – Anna Parnell
Donigan – Anna Parnell/Joe Beers
Goldrush – Jessica Page/Valentina Hirsch
MidnightInVerona – Jessica Page/Valentina Hirsch
Paladin – Jessica Page/Valentina Hirsch
Songster – Marcy Katz/Darrell Manning

I hesitated over Donigan and almost gave up the project altogether but decided to soldier on. If anyone asked why my name was on there, I'd say I was the responsible party for now and leave it at that. I'd never met Songster's owner, Darrell Manning, I realized. He'd never come out while Marcy was doing her training, and I wondered if he was even in the area. Perhaps he lived elsewhere and just enjoyed his horses vicariously. A lot of wealthy owners did that. Hired a good trainer and then just stepped away.

What would it be like to have that much money? There was a part of me that wondered, and another part that couldn't figure out why you'd own a beautiful horse and then have no interest in being around it or watching it in the show ring? I shrugged. Being fabulously wealthy was not something I was likely to ever have to worry about.

When I headed for the barn carrying my newly-printed, carefully-formatted sign, Jessica's BMW was in the parking area and Paladin was standing in crossties, ready to be ridden. Jessica lifted the saddle over his back.

"Morning," she called when I walked by, and then followed me to inspect my sign. "Good idea," she said. "Almost Esther. Is she entered at KHE?"

"Um, no. I'm treating her for an abscess. I might go in one of the shows later in the summer if she's going well enough."

"She nickered at me when I walked by. Pretty mare. She reminds me of a mare I saw for sale down in Asheville. What a nice horse. I think she sold for over one-fifty. She was an open jumper. RubyTuesday, d'you know her?"

I shook my head.

"I'm a little surprised I haven't seen her over at the showgrounds. I know the guy who bought her. He said he'd be starting her at the KHE Special."

"Esther and I are aiming for dressage," I said,

choosing to avoid commenting on the astonishing price of $150,000 Jessica had tossed out like it was nothing. I wasn't disclosing to anyone the pittance I'd paid for Esther, and I was sure she was worth five times what RubyTuesday cost. She was very definitely my heart horse. I put the last pushpin in my poster, and just then Jason walked up.

"I didn't give permission for my name to be broadcast all over the place," he said coldly. "Let's get that taken down." He reached out but I intercepted his hand and pushed it away, wondering at my boldness. I wasn't prone to touching people like that, but Jason ... honestly.

Struggling to keep my voice calm, I answered. "It's just horse names and owner-trainer names. Let's *not* take it down."

I noticed Jessica was edging away.

"It's private information," Jason responded.

"Not so private. Just horse names and people names," I repeated.

"Also, I don't like the kick pads you hung in AllBeCalm's stall. I need him moved." Jason appeared to have turned his ire elsewhere and I had to give myself a shake to re-direct my attention to his next complaint.

Jason was carrying a short riding crop, and he slapped it against his hand. I took a deep breath, struggling for control. "Your horse kicks the wall. Without the pads, I'm afraid he'll injure himself. If you want to request a different stall, I'm happy to move him, but you'll have to put your wishes in writing. Liability, you know." I kept my hand on the sign in case he made another run at pulling it down, and looked steadily at Jason, daring him to push the issue of finding Mayhem another stall.

Jason seemed to hesitate. "Those pads are a hazard," he finally snapped, then turned on his heel and walked away, shooting, "I'll put that in writing," over his shoulder.

I closed my eyes. I hated how my insecurities took over at times like these. Cameron would give me a lecture on how much horse experience I had, and why I shouldn't let Jason rattle me. *You know about kick pads and how to install them. Don't let Jason get under your skin.* I could hear my husband saying it, but it was hard not to take things to heart. I decided to sneak into Mayhem's stall and confirm that there was nothing to injure him. I was sure there wasn't, but Jason's belligerence aside, I didn't want anything to harm his horse. It didn't hurt to check.

Jessica was leading Paladin out to the jump arena as I left the barn, seething inwardly. She shot a look at Jason, who was leading AllBeCalm to the wash stand, exchanged a look with me, and rolled her eyes.

"He's a jerk," she commented under her breath. "Marcy and I have known him from way back."

I didn't respond, because it would have been impolitic for me to do so, but oh, did I want to!

Instead, I gave Jessica a little smile and went into the house. Then I sat down, took a deep breath to settle my nerves, and phoned Elsa.

"I'm glad you called!" Elsa cried. "How is Donagin?"

"Not much different today," I answered. "He'd like to go out, but he's such a gentleman he is just standing quietly in his stall and not making any sort of a fuss. It's like he knows he needs to be quiet. Joe did a good job with him," I added, and waited while Elsa steadied her voice.

Finally, "Good," she said, and there was a long silence.

"I shipped Joe's things off to you via UPS," I said. "They promised they would have them to you within three days."

"Thank you!" Elsa exclaimed. "What's in the boxes?"

"Not all that much, actually. A couple of articles of clothing, some saddle pads, brushes, a few personal items ..." I decided not to mention the flask. "... a packet of papers."

"Papers? What sort of papers?" Elsa had picked up right away on the unusual thing.

"Well, I didn't look too carefully," I sort-of lied. "One was a showbill for the KHE. A ledger sheet ..."

Elsa jumped on that. "A ledger sheet? What for?"

"Looked like for a sale horse?" I was getting increasingly uncomfortable, and wished for all the world I hadn't looked at that wretched paper.

"You didn't take a cell pic of it by any chance, did you?" Elsa asked quickly.

"No, I didn't." I was finally able to be completely truthful. "I just put everything I found in the box and sent it to you. I've got Donagin's saddle and bridle here, and I can send those if you like. But I thought it might be better to hold onto them if I'm going to rehab Donagin, so he has tack he's used to—"

Elsa cut me off. "Oh yes, keep the bridle and saddle." I shook my head, thinking of the cost of those items. I wished I could say, *Oh yes, keep them*, to someone about my tack, which I'd bought second hand and probably for less money than Joe had paid for Donagin's bit.

I'm getting obsessed about money, I thought

suddenly. *I need to stop this.*

"The reason I'm interested in the ledger," Elsa said, and I wrenched my mind away from expensive saddles back to the conversation. "Is that we sold a horse to someone, and the buyer hasn't paid up. It was sort of a lease or try-out deal, but it's way past the deadline. Joe was going to talk to the buyer at the showgrounds, but of course ..."

"Of course," I murmured, trying to decide what to say and again wishing I'd just stuffed all those papers into a bag without looking at them.

But Elsa saved me by going on. "The buyer is someone named Jason Barlowe. I've got so much on my hands here that I haven't been able to do anything, but later this week I'm contacting my attorney. I don't know for sure how much he owes, but if the ledger sheet has the balance, I'll have what I need to go after him."

"Jason Barlowe! He's got a horse here," I said, glad once again to be able to stick with what was true. "A horse called AllBeCalm."

"AllBeCalm! That's the one we sold him!" All of a sudden Elsa's bubbly, friendly voice didn't sound quite so bubbly and friendly. "He's got the nerve to show up where Joe had Donagin? I can't believe it. He's the worst sort, Annie. He'll cheat you. You need to steer clear of him."

I grimaced and decided to stay quiet. Jason had paid six weeks' board in advance. His check had cleared. Okay, yes, I'd had to buy kick pads because of his horse's miserable habits, but that was what my business required. What was I supposed to do?

Elsa sounded for all the world as if she was grinding her teeth. "Oh, that ... that ..." She seemed at a loss for words, and I gently cut in.

"If there's anything else I can do, let me know. I'll start emailing you daily progress reports on Donagin, and of course I'll send you the vet notes."

But Elsa wasn't done. "I mean it, Annie. Stay away from him. I think Joe was a little afraid of him."

"Okay," I said weakly. Joe Beers was *afraid* of Jason Barlowe? I didn't like this turn in the conversation at all. How did Elsa know that?

Elsa and I ended our call, and I went back out to the barn, my feet dragging. Unfortunately, I felt a bit afraid of Jason myself. When he got into one of his tirades, he was downright intimidating, and it seemed to me as if he just walked around looking for a way to vent his spleen.

I sighed loudly.

Jessica was in the arena schooling Paladin and I saw her take a spectacular jump, Paladin's coat shining in the sun like a copper penny. My mind turned from debts and Jason and other problems I couldn't control. The reason I'd wanted to open Catalpa was that I loved horses, and being close to the KHE was just perfect. There would be a lot of talented animals there, and I was excited about seeing it all once the show got underway.

I walked into the barn and stopped short in the barn aisle. There was a figure standing in front of AllBeCalm's stall. A figure that was stroking with gentle patience the face of the horse I called Mayhem.

Mayhem had his wicked eyes half closed and was leaning into the hand of the person caressing him. That person was Jason Barlowe.

Chapter Eleven

And then Valentina Hirsch arrived.

Marcy was hosing off Songster and Jessica had just put MidnightInVerona in the crossties when there was a commotion out in the circle drive, and Esther, whom I was grooming, startled. Ron ran past me, his tail the size of a milk bottle, Hermione close behind. My cats scooted into the tack room, and I saw Ron poke one cautious yellow eye around the corner.

I tossed down the brush I was using and strode to the barn door to see what was happening, noticing an exchange of wry glances between Jessica and Marcy.

Valentina—it had to be she—was just shutting off the engine of her Porsche, which killed the sound of the music blasting through the speakers. Some sort of pop, perhaps. I didn't recognize the artist, but the volume was so loud that it was hard to tell exactly what was playing.

She took off her sunglasses and shot me a brilliant smile as I approached her from the barn. I made a split-second decision not to mention that she might try playing her music with fewer decibels. I'd take a *wait and see* attitude, in case this was an anomaly.

"Annie, I presume?" she said in her lilting voice, sounding just like a Southern belle. "I'm Valentina. Sorry if I disturbed you. I do like mah music." She put her sunglasses up on her head and held out her hand.

She was a lovely woman. Slim and athletic in riding breeches and leather driving gloves of paper-thin, buff leather. Her dark hair was long and curling and pulled away from her face with a silver barrette.

"Yes, I'm Annie," I answered. "I hope you had a good trip?"

"Oh, travel makes m'bones ache a bit, but you know," she smiled at me conspiratorially. "We keep on keepin' on, don't we?" Her eyes fell on Midnight, who was striding out of the barn alongside Jessica. Valentina moved past me. "How's it goin', honey?" she called to Jessica. "How're mah horses doin'?"

Jessica pulled Midnight to a halt. "Hi, Valentina. I've already worked Paladin and I was just about to ride Midnight here. D'you want to—" But Valentina's eyes had moved past Jessica, traveling down the row of paddocks.

She turned back to me. "You've got a mighty pretty place here, Annie. How many horses?"

"Seven as of right now."

"An' how many do you hold?"

"I can take as many as twelve at one time. Hoping to have at least twenty cycle through during the KHE Special."

"Let's take a look at the stalls." Jessica continued leading Midnight to the arena and Valentina strode toward the barn with me trailing behind. She started down the row of stalls and gave Goldrush a light pat on the nose. "I do like this mare," she said over her shoulder, and then stopped at Donagin. "And who do we have here? Are you hurt handsome fella?" I didn't have to answer because she turned back to me. "Is this the horse that poor man was riding when he fell? I heard about that over at Keystone. Seems like everyone's talkin' about it." Valentina's pretty face was scrunched in sympathy. Donagin watched us from his hay mow, chewing slowly.

"Are they?" I asked. "Talking? Yes, this is the horse. It was a terrible accident."

"It surely was," she agreed. "So sad."

Valentina strode on, walked past Esther without a second glance, and then came back. "I'm thinking of scratching Paladin from the show," she commented suddenly. "He just isn't going how I'd like, and there's no point in entering if we can't take home a win. Jessica'll be disappointed. She loves that horse. But ..." Valentina gave a light shrug of her shoulders.

"I'm sorry to hear that." *For several reasons*, I thought. *I was depending on that income!* "When will you be moving him?"

"Oh, I'll leave him here. We'll ship all the horses out when the hunter classes are over. Who else is boarding here right now?" Her eye fell on my sign. "Marcy Katz. Yes. She's ridin' for Darrell Manning now, is she? I'd heard she and J. D. had a falling out."

"Oh," I began. "I don't know—"

"J. D. Williams. He's got two, or is it three now, I can't remember, Trakehner horses. Marcy's a good rider, but ..." Valentina gave a dismissive wave. "J. D.'s kind of out of her league."

I wasn't listening very carefully. *J. D. Williams. J. D. Williams. Where had I heard that name?*

"I mean," Valentina chattered, "Last time he was in Europe I thought he'd blow a fuse, and I mean *blow a fuse* when Gabriela Framingham showed up with her Dutch horse and beat him by just a few points. He just went crazy. Was Marcy with him then? I can't remember for sure. Seems like I can't remember much of anythin' these days!" Valentina giggled. "J. D.'s always got his eye on the competition. There's an edge to him that's somethin' to see, all right. Marcy just doesn't have his *drive*."

I was only half listening. I was still racking my brain for the name J. D. Williams. Suddenly I got it. The blonde man who had been at the fence line while Officer Lopez was here. Why *had* he been there? Was he thinking of checking out Catalpa as a boarding facility, or was he scoping out who was in the barns, or was it just morbid curiosity?

Valentina turned away from the board and swept outside, and I found myself once more following in her wake. The woman had a personality, that was for sure. It was as if she absorbed all the available energy. She stopped just outside the door and folded her arms, watching Jessica and Midnight circle the arena, take a low fence and then follow up with a triple.

Midnight looked amazing, her front legs perfectly tucked and her ears forward as if she was jumping for the sheer fun of it. It was a treat to watch.

"They're blowing the depart," Valentina murmured, and I looked at her with surprise. They *were?* I was no expert, but I thought they looked spectacular. Then Valentina called out, "Jessica, honey!" Jessica glanced over and pulled Midnight down to a trot, then a walk. They rode up to the fence, and Jessica looked inquiringly at Valentina. Valentina gazed critically at Midnight as they approached. "Honey, I'm going to scratch Paladin. He's not right for the KHE crowd. Focus your attention on Goldrush and Midnight, and work on Midnight's take off. She's a half-stride late."

I saw several emotions cross Jessica's face.

Surprise, displeasure, and resignation, followed by a flash of repugnance—what was that about?—and then Jessica said, "Oh, but—"

Valentina held up a hand and Jessica fell silent. "Let's don't go on about this," she said. "I've made up mah mind. Daniel Martin's got Manderley entered in the same classes as Paladin. No and no. I don't want what happened the last time those two went up against each other. No, I've made up my mind. Paladin's out."

Jessica didn't protest this time. She just gazed steadily at Valentina and said, "Whatever you think."

I debated whether I could slink away and let the two of them talk privately, but Valentina turned to me, pulling her sunglasses down and twirling them before perching them back on her nose. "Well, I'm headin' off," she said cheerily, as if she didn't notice Jessica looking like the bottom had just dropped out of her world. "I've got to find a place to stay. Mah hotel reservations got confused, and I'm in a room that won't do." She strode off toward her car.

I looked up at Jessica on Midnight, but her face was now unreadable. She picked up the mare's reins and turned her back toward the jump course.

As for me, I returned to the barn and hurried gratefully to Esther so I could finish grooming her and wrap her foot. She'd been waiting in the crossties for what seemed like forever. I hadn't meant to leave her for so long, but Valentina ... she was like a hurricane.

Esther had been standing like the good girl she was, but she gave me what I feared was a bit of a scolding look, so I slipped her a treat and finished grooming her, taking special care to use the soft bristle brush she particularly liked. Then I inspected her abscessed foot, glad that Crystal was going to look at it, and took my mare to her paddock.

Back out in the arena, MidnightInVerona and Jessica were circling, taking the coup jump, the triple, and the low wall, but to my eyes it seemed as if some of the joy had gone out of it.

Chapter Twelve

I texted Cameron to see if we could have another visit to the DZ, so we met on the deck after he got home from school and I poured us each a glass of wine.

I'd finished the before-dinner chores—bringing all the horses in from their paddocks and making sure everyone had hay and their evening measure of grain, so it was nice to kick back for a few minutes and have some quiet time with my husband.

"They're all characters," I said to Cameron, thinking of the people with horses at Catalpa. "Every single one of them."

Cameron nodded. "I suppose everyone is. Are their odd behaviors causing problems?"

I leaned back in my chair and looked up at the sky, which was gray and rainy looking. "Not really. They're just an interesting bunch. All of them different. They all seem to know each other in one way or another. It turns out Jessica Page and Marcy Katz are thick as thieves. They always have their heads together about something. Valentina Hirsch—that's Jessica's boss—what a trip! And Jason Barlowe. At least I didn't need to worry about any run-ins with him today. He came out last night to work Mayhem when everyone was done for the day and evening chores finished, and I haven't seen him today." I shook my head.

Cameron furrowed his brow. "He shouldn't be doing that, should he? I wouldn't think it would be very safe without arena lights."

"True. I'm going to have to look into lights, and I suppose they'll cost a small fortune." I frowned. "But he did ride before it got dark. I think he's just antisocial. Avoiding everyone. With the new horses and people here, it's too crowded." I gave a small smile. "He started his evening routine after Valentina's horses came."

Cameron looked at me questioningly.

I cleared my throat. "I dunno. It's as if there's some undercurrent, and I don't know what it is. Like secrets or something."

"Secrets. Hmm." Cameron swirled his glass of wine.

"I'm probably making that up. There's just a weird vibe sometimes."

"A weird vibe. That's rather non-specific."

"It's likely my imagination." I shrugged. "On another note, though, I'm wondering about some barn rules. I've been thinking about a list. Hours, maybe? Where people should park their cars? Valentina came rolling in here with her music at top volume. I suppose it could have scared the horses, although this time it didn't seem to do any harm. Also, I need to hang some No Trespassing signs on the fence line between us and the KHE."

"Because of the guy who showed up while the police were here?"

"Yes. I don't like the idea of people wandering around on the cross-country course. Valentina knows him, it turns out. And also Marcy. Marcy used to work for him, but it sounds as if he fired her."

"Why?"

"I'm not sure. Valentina mentioned it. Something about his horses and how she trained and rode them. It was a little vague."

Cameron nodded slowly. "You're right. They all seem to know each other, one way or another. And sometimes not in a good way."

"The guy at the fence was J. D. Williams. I think that's his name. Valentina mentioned him and I finally remembered that he'd introduced himself when we saw him. Took me a while to remember."

"Are you having any trouble with Marcy?"

I shook my head. "Not at all. I like her, although it seems like she sort of kept to herself until Valentina's three horses came in. Then she was here for most of the afternoon after Jessica came, and the two of them left together. Oh yes, and I talked with Elsa Kurchner."

"Joe Beers's widow, right?"

"Right. Well, she warned me to stay *way* away from Jason Barlowe. Said that he'd cheat me, and I don't know what all. It was a bit chilling."

Cameron sat up straight. "This is the guy who is avoiding you?"

"I don't know if he's avoiding me or avoiding Jessica or just avoiding everyone. He's not a pleasant guy to be around, that's for sure. He's just ... I don't know ... abrasive. But he's all paid up for the time he's got AllBeCalm here. I have no evidence that he's cheating me out of anything. Yet Elsa doesn't like him. She knew about him buying AllBeCalm from Joe, by the way. And that he hasn't paid up, so I'm sure that's why the bad blood. That and his charming personality."

Cameron made a face. "It sounds like a giant soap opera."

I didn't answer. Cameron was right.

"How is Esther's foot?" he asked.

"I'm going to have Crystal take a look at it. It may be time to see if we can drain the abscess." We sat quietly for a couple of minutes. "And another thing," I said suddenly.

Cameron smiled. "What?"

"I'm wondering when the police are going to wrap up their investigation of Joe's death. I'd like to know what they're doing and if they have any suspects. Partly I'd just like to know, and partly I'd like to open up the cross-country course. I'm not sure if I should cut a new trail? I know if I do, it'll be right when they take the barrier tape down. Is there more evidence to look for, or what?" I frowned. "No one's likely to be using those jumps for anything but schooling right now, since there is no cross-country competition at the Special. But still. It would be nice to know what is going on. And to be able to use the north trail again for when the smaller shows come through. They'll do short cross-country classes."

We sat in silence for a little while and gazed out into the gathering evening. I stole a look at Cameron. He seemed relaxed and happy—far from what I would be if my wife had a huge farm venture and persisted in unloading all her worries on me, *and* I was in law school with all that stress on my mind.

"I better go check the barn and let you get at your studying," I said at last. "Thanks for listening."

"Absolutely no problem. We should plan a date night. Let's see what live music is around. Get away for an evening."

"I'd like that," I said.

Cameron disappeared into his office, and I went out to the barn to do a final check on all the horses. I paused by Paladin's stall and wondered what had made Valentina decide to scratch him from the show. He was gorgeous, he seemed to jump everything he was pointed at, and his form over the jumps with Jessica astride was perfect, as best I could tell. Was Valentina thinking perhaps she couldn't handle Paladin when it came time for her to climb aboard? Or maybe she wasn't planning to ride him at all, and Jessica would have been the one to take him into the ring. Oh well. It was sad for Jessica, but Valentina got to call the shots.

I walked around to check on Esther and give her a nighttime flake of hay, then wandered down the last aisle.

I was surprised to find AllBeCalm wasn't in his stall, and I hurried to look out at the arena.

Sure enough, Jason and Mayhem were there circling the ring. Jason must have driven in while Cameron and I were in the DZ. I'd told Cameron that Jason didn't ride after dark, and it wasn't dark, but it was going to be there soon. I wondered again about some barn rules, and again wondered what lights for the arena would cost. I should get some, for safety's sake, if nothing else.

Jason is a very good rider, I thought as I watched. *Quiet and giving in the saddle*. He took Mayhem over some low rails and steadied him nicely, then steadied him again when the horse let out some explosive bucks. I could just hear his quiet voice soothing his excited mount, and although I couldn't make out what he said, I saw AllBeCalm balance himself, his ears flicking back and forth as Jason's words flowed over him.

They took the wall and two more rail jumps, then Jason eased him to a trot and to a walk. He bent to pat his horse's shoulder, then offered him something—a bit of carrot perhaps, or a sugar lump. It was obviously something AllBeCalm expected, because he'd stretched his head around for his treat before Jason's hand had gone to his pocket.

Interesting, I thought. *Interesting.*

Jason Barlowe, who seemed to hate everyone, whom Elsa Kurchner had labeled "the worst sort," who appeared to have defaulted on a large payment, and who had been inexcusably rude to me, really had a way with animals. My cats adored him, and apparently the renegade horse AllBeCalm could be made to behave and to become a competitive show animal under his guiding hands.

It didn't make me like Jason any better, but it did make me curious. What kind of a man was he, anyway?

Chapter Thirteen

Crystal had an opening just before lunchtime. She said she'd check out Esther and also take a look at Donagin, whom I had been carefully hand-walking around the arena every day.

I kissed Cameron goodbye and did the morning chores, then spent some time sweeping and cobwebbing and thinking about a system for arena lighting. LED lamps with a dark/light sensor seemed as if it was the way to go.

I had just finished the sweeping when I heard voices and Jessica and Marcy came striding down the far aisle, talking in low tones. They stopped speaking when they turned the corner and saw me, then Marcy raised a hand in hello, and they continued on their way. I had the feeling they'd halted their conversation because they didn't wish me to hear. I shrugged.

Soon they brought Songster and Goldrush inside to be saddled, and I went about my own business, finishing my tidying up, grooming Esther, and snuggling with my Harry Potter trio of cats in the tack room.

After a while, I heard Marcy and Jessica coming back in from their rides, then Jessica left to put Goldrush back out and fetch Midnight.

A moment later Marcy came into the tack room,

and I looked at her curiously. She was carrying Songster's bridle, but held the reins in a tangle, running them through her fingers as if she were agitated or upset.

"Hey," she greeted me, and I smiled. "Have a minute?" she went on.

I stood, gave Ron a last pat, and watched him scamper away, then brushed off the seat of my jeans. "Sure," I said. "What's up?"

Marcy hung Songster's bridle on its hook and then peeked out the tack room door, making sure we couldn't be overheard, I presumed. I waited, wondering what the cloak and dagger routine was about.

"Um." Marcy shifted her feet and twisted her fingers together. "You aren't planning to bring any of J. D.'s horses in, are you?"

"J. D. Williams, you mean?" Marcy nodded. "Not to my knowledge. No one's contacted me about it, anyway. Why do you ask?"

Marcy looked over her shoulder again. "Valentina said something about it to Jessica and Jessica told me."

"Oh," I said. "Then Valentina knows something I don't know. I've only met J. D. Williams once, and that was when he hiked over from the KHE and was standing at the back fence during ... when the police were here."

Marcy made an angry gesture. "That sounds like J. D. He's a snoopy ... He's very snoopy." She paced the room, stopping at the saddles and then turning to face me. She took a deep breath. "It's just that if you're thinking of boarding J. D.'s horses here ... That is, if he asks about bringing some horses to Catalpa, I hope you don't do it."

I hesitated, unsure what to say. I couldn't very easily turn down a paying customer, but I also didn't need drama and contention among the riders.

Marcy rushed on. "I used to work for him, you know." I nodded and Marcy made a wry face. "I'm sure everyone knows. It's awful. He and I ..." She sighed. "It's complicated. He and I sort of got involved. You don't want to hear all this, I know. He's such a good-looking guy, and he's got all these beautiful horses. I never should have done it. It got very messy, and ultimately, he fired me. Not because of my riding or anything, but because of our relationship." I stared at her, at a loss for words. Marcy sighed and I saw tears gather in her eyes. "I know this is all TMI. Too Much Information, but it's important to me, and I want you to understand. I told him I was going to stop seeing him, and he didn't want to, and ... well ... he was my boss, and ... and ..." A tear slid down her face. "When I didn't relent, he let me go. For a while I was sort of ... I don't know, maybe blackballed. I couldn't get another training job anywhere, and I think J. D. probably had something to do with that. He was furious when I broke it off. Then Darrell Manning hired me, and it's worked out okay. I try to avoid J. D., but it's hard since we show in the same circuit. But if he brings his horses here, I just don't know what I'm going to do."

I hesitated. After that tale, I wasn't inclined to have anything to do with J. D. He had to be twice Marcy's age, and I guessed there was more Marcy wasn't telling me about what had happened, none of it good. Besides, I'd grown to like Marcy, and I was certain she was understating what had happened. The truth was likely far uglier. Finally, I said, "I understand."

A flash of anger crossed Marcy's face. "I'm not sure you do. Jessica told me Valentina's out to get one of J. D.'s horses. A very nice jumper. A Trakehner that J. D.

imported from Europe last year. She's trying to talk him down in price, and she's—" Marcy shook her head. "Jessica says she's sleeping with him." A tear ran down Marcy's cheek. "*Please* don't tell Jessica I told you. She'd be so angry. I just don't want J. D. around here. I don't like him, and I don't trust him."

I grimaced. "I *do* understand, Marcy. Will Valentina get what she wants? The horse, that is? Sounds as if she had better be careful, based on your experience."

Marcy clenched her fist against her knee. "Who knows? She's not exactly an angel herself. I know at least three other people she's been with. And I'm pretty sure that's how she got Goldrush. By sleeping with a guy over in Germany."

"Good grief," I said.

Marcy lifted one shoulder to wipe away the tear that had slid down. "Please don't tell Jessica," she repeated.

"I won't," I promised. "J. D. sounds like a womanizer. He doesn't have any history with Jessica, does he?" I clapped my hand over my mouth. "Never mind, that's none of my business."

Marcy gave a half smile. "It's okay. Um, no. Jessica's got no interest in J. D. She's got a girlfriend back in Kentucky. Jessica just doesn't want to get on Valentina's bad side. Valentina's not an easy person to work for, and she pulled Paladin out from under Jessica. She's afraid she'll lose another horse if Valentina thinks she's talking behind her back."

"I get it," I said. "I appreciate you telling me because this sort of tangle is not something I want to deal with. It's enough work looking after the horses. Thanks for the warning about J. D. I'll keep it in mind." I couldn't very well promise her not to take his horses, but I'd heard enough that I was convinced having J. D. around Catalpa was going to be a negative rather than a positive.

Marcy nodded at me, wiped away another tear, schooled her face, and walked out into the aisle. Soon I heard her laughing at something Jessica had said, and I left the tack room for Esther's paddock to wait for Crystal to arrive. And to think. A lot.

Crystal checked out Esther's hoof and looked over the area where we knew the abscess was lurking. "You know, I think this is ready to break through," she said, eyeing the hoof and tilting it upward and then down toward the ground. "There may already be a little opening here. Let's just see if we can open it the rest of the way up and give this girl some relief." Esther turned her head and stared at Crystal, and I gave my horse a pat on the neck.

Crystal fetched a hoof knife from her truck, lifted Esther's foot again, and gently pared away a small area of the sole. Suddenly Esther gave a start and Crystal said, "Therrrre we go. How does that feel, pretty Esther?" Crystal looked up at me. "This is draining now, and she should be doing great in a few days. We just need to keep it from getting infected while the hoof grows back." I nodded and watched as Crystal applied a medicated pad and wrapped the hoof. "You'll want a waterproof boot on this," she commented, and I held up the one I had in my hand. "Great." She slid it on and let Esther stand on the affected leg.

I was delighted to see that my horse's pain seemed to have diminished substantially now that the pressure of the abscess was gone. Crystal gestured at Esther's foot. "You just want to keep this clean and dry and watch for when it stops draining. Then it should be business as usual!" She patted Esther and smiled as Esther picked up a mouthful of hay and began to chew. "Now, shall we look at Donagin?"

"Yes, let's," I said. I glanced around to be sure we weren't being overheard. "Crystal, do you know J. D. Williams?"

Crystal snorted. "J. D. Williams. You mean the blonde bombshell of the KHE? That J. D. Williams?"

I laughed. "I think that's the one."

Crystal shrugged. "Yeah, I know him. Half the people at the KHE have a crush on him—both women and men. He's got quite the fan club. It isn't surprising, I suppose. He looks like a fashion model, but he appears to have the morals of an alley cat. He has a fantastic string of horses, that's for sure."

"Okay, that matches what I've heard," I said. "Someone shared with me today that he's not above using his position to pressure his employees. He seems like a creep."

"Owes a lot of money, too," Crystal added. "He's got a gambling problem, I hear. I'm not sure what people see in him."

"Owes a lot of money … must be something in the air," I said sourly. "This is between the two of us, okay?" Crystal made a zipping motion across her mouth. "Jason Barlowe, the man who rides AllBeCalm? Apparently, the horse doesn't exactly belong to him. AllBeCalm was a 'try out', and he owes the buy price on him. I found it out sort of by accident."

Crystal shook her head. "Lots of high rollers in the horse show world, but some of them can't afford to be. That's an odd try out agreement, though. Normally, I wouldn't have thought an owner would let someone take a horse to a competition when it was on try out."

"I'm not sure," I mused. "And I don't know the real story with the agreement. Joe Beers is the one who owned, or maybe still owns, AllBeCalm—"

"Joe Beers?" Crystal interrupted. "The man who was killed?"

"The very one."

"'Curiouser and curiouser,'" Crystal quipped. "I wonder what's going to happen now?"

"Hard to know. It sounds as if his wife is going to go after the money. I can't blame her at all. Jason owes her a barrel of cash. It's kind of a mess. But, at least so far as I know, Jason isn't sleeping with half the universe. Or if he is, no one's mentioned it."

"There's not a person on the KHE grounds who doesn't know about J. D. Williams and his shenanigans," Crystal said.

She walked up the barn aisle with me trailing along behind her and stopped at Donagin's stall. "Look at you, standing on that foot!" she exclaimed. She slid open the stall door and bent to feel Donagin's ankle with practiced fingers, checking for heat and tenderness. Finally, she stood. "I'm going to ultrasound him again, just to be sure, but I'm thinking we should keep up the hand-walking for a few more days. If things go well, he can be ridden at the walk. He's got a ways to go, but he's making good progress."

"That's a relief," I said.

"He's a beautiful horse," Crystal said. "I wonder what's going to happen to him?"

"I'm not sure," I answered honestly. "Joe's wife has got her hands full, and she asked if I'd continue with his rehab, which I'm happy to do. But she'll have to make a decision about him eventually. She mentioned moving him back down to Florida. I'm wondering if she'll end up selling him."

"Whoever gets him will have quite the prize. Injury or no injury. My gut's telling me this guy is going to come back mostly sound."

"He's just an amazing horse, both in talent and in behavior. I've never handled such a sensible animal. Except Esther, of course," I added, and Crystal grinned.

I thought of J. D. Williams and Valentina angling to get one of his Trakehners. Did J. D. need money badly enough to let one of his prize horses go for less than it was worth? It seemed Valentina would want the horse as a show animal, but what would J. D. be willing to do for money? If he had the gambling debts Crystal thought he had, who knew? I'd do anything in my power to keep Donagin from becoming part of a trade like that.

"Wow! That was quite a scowl!" Crystal exclaimed. "What on earth were you thinking about?"

I winced. "Was I scowling? Sorry. I was just thinking about some of the ugly undercurrents around here."

"Ugly undercurrents?" Crystal asked.

I hesitated. The vision of Joe's dead body had swum before my eyes.

I shrugged, and Crystal patted me on the shoulder. "I'm sure everything will sort itself out. Joe's death doesn't mean the end of Catalpa. Not by a long shot."

"I hope not," I said in a small voice. "I really, really do."

Chapter Fourteen

I walked with Crystal back to her truck and stood leaning against the door as my friend grabbed a granola bar and downed it in two bites. "That's quite a lunch you have there," I commented.

Crystal laughed. "I've got an apple in here somewhere. Hopefully, it didn't roll away."

She peered under a jacket lying on the seat and then transferred her attention to the floor. I sighed and she glanced over her shoulder at me. "What's the matter?"

I grimaced. "I've got sort of a bad feeling."

Crystal stopped rummaging under her truck seat, spied her apple on the dashboard, and grabbed it, rubbing it against her shirt front. "What about?"

"About how things are going, I guess. I know you think I shouldn't worry about this being the end of Catalpa, but I still can't get over Joe Beers dying like that."

"Well, that's not surprising. Who would?"

"And then there's Joe's wife warning me away from Jason Barlowe, and Marcy warning me away from J. D. Williams."

"I agree with Marcy on that one," Crystal said. "That guy is bad news." She stuffed her apple into a paper bag.

"Am I attracting a bad crowd do you think?" I mused.

"Nah." Crystal climbed in and started up her truck. "Most of the show people are perfectly fine. Jason hasn't been a problem for you. His money issues aren't your issues, right? And you don't have to deal with J. D. He's got his horses at the KHE and they can stay there perfectly well."

"From what Marcy said, it sounds as if Valentina's been pushing him to bring a couple of them over here. I'm not sure why she cares, you know?"

Crystal shrugged. "Well, maybe it'll never happen. And if he asks, turn him down. Tell him you've got two horses rehabbing—which you do—and don't have stall space or bandwidth for any more. My guess is this'll all go away once the show starts. J. D. won't want to be messing with moving to a new venue once the competition is underway."

"You're probably right. Thanks, Crystal."

"You're welcome. Call me anytime." Crystal smiled, put her truck in gear, and maneuvered around the circle drive onto the main road, waving to me out her open window.

I walked back up to the barn, deep in thought. The problem wasn't J. D. or whatever Jason's money issues were, it was Joe. The idea of someone being killed on my jump course was haunting me. Especially *how* they were killed. If my suspicions were true, and I had to assume that they were, since there was enough evidence for the police to launch an investigation, then there was a murderer somewhere close by. It wasn't a happy thought.

I wished I knew how the inquiry was going. Had

they discovered anything else? Worse, was there any way I was on the list of suspects? It was frustrating to be out of the loop.

My day wasn't brightened when I phoned Elsa with what I thought was good news about Donagin's progress, only to find she was in tears again.

"I'm sorry, Annie," she said at last. "I'm so distracted and upset I just don't know what to do."

"What's happened?" I asked.

I heard Elsa take a deep breath. "Well, I've been getting calls on my phone from a blocked number. I always get some—the usual political calls or scams or whatever—but in the last few days they've been increasing by a lot. I've been letting them go to voicemail, but whoever it is always hangs up. Then yesterday, I decided to answer one just to see what was going on, and someone spoke to me. Elsa paused. It sounded as if she was trying to settle her breathing. They said 'Be very, very careful. You don't want to end up like your husband, do you?'"

"Oh no!" I gasped. "Did you call the police?"

"Of course. They're working on tracing the number. But then today I got a letter. A threatening letter. Basically telling me if I took AllBeCalm back, I'd be very sorry."

"What!" I exclaimed. "Do you have any idea who is doing this?"

"None. I don't even know if the same person called and wrote the letter. Although I suspect it is. It's just awful."

"Was it a man or a woman on the phone?"

"I couldn't tell," Elsa said. "Whoever it was, I think they were disguising their voice to sound deep and sinister. It sounded sort of fake, to tell you the truth, but

I still have no idea who it might have been."

"But," I protested. "But the only person who has any claim to AllBeCalm is Jason Barlowe, right?"

"I know," Elsa said in a low voice. "Have you seen him around?"

"Well, yes," I said. "He's prepping for the Keystone Horse Exhibition and he rides every day for a couple of hours. Usually in the late afternoon or evening."

"I don't suppose you've noticed anything unusual?"

I shrugged. "No, not really. I haven't even talked to him lately. I guess the only unusual thing is that he's sort of changed his riding habits. He used to come out earlier in the day, but I thought … I don't know, I thought maybe he was trying to avoid the other riders. He's not much of a people person."

"I know he isn't," Elsa said. "In fact, he's a horrible man. And I wouldn't put it past him at all to think he's going to get some sort of special treatment because I've lost … lost my husband," Elsa continued in a trembling voice. "I'm nearly sure he's the one that's doing this. I can't imagine who else it would be. And if someone murdered Joe, the police should know about Jason."

I took a quick look over my shoulder, just as if Jason might be creeping up on me. There was no one there. The barn was quiet and empty and probably would be for the next couple of hours. Then Marcy and Jessica would likely show up and things would be hopping while they put their mounts through their practice for the upcoming show.

"I'm going to tell the police about him," Elsa's angry voice cut into my thoughts. "I wasn't sure I should, but they need to know about my suspicions. I'm so tired of this! As if I didn't have enough, with ..." she couldn't go on, and I heard her begin to sob. "Can I call you back, Annie?"

"Of course." I clicked off my phone and started slowly for the house and my lunch break, wishing there was something I could do, and very much wishing I could get Jason Barlowe and AllBeCalm out of my barn. How could he threaten a grieving woman like that? It was one of the most heartless acts I'd ever heard.

Not as bad as murdering Joe, of *course, but ...*

Someone had put a rope across the cross-country trail and tripped Donagin as he'd taken the ramp jump. Donagin had fallen, spilling Joe off his back. The fall had killed a fine man and lamed his fine horse.

Was Jason responsible? Had he somehow thought he could get out from under his huge debt if he killed the person to whom he owed the money?

But as Cameron had pointed out, the debt would be part of the estate, and he'd still owe Elsa. There had to be some other reason. Unless ... unless he didn't think Elsa knew about the debt. Didn't know about the ledger sheet Joe Beers had kept. Didn't know I'd sent it to her. I felt a chill run down my arms.

But for a sum like that, Jason had to assume Joe had some records. There should have been an agreement between the two men, allowing Jason to try out AllBeCalm for a specified period and then pay off the balance due. Wouldn't Jason know that once Elsa sorted through Joe's papers, the debt would come to light?

I felt very, very sorry for Elsa. To lose her husband would be bad enough without all this. I had a sudden urge to call Cameron, but I knew he would be in class. Then I thought about sending him a text just to say hello, but I was afraid he might think something was wrong. Which it was, but also wasn't.

My shoulders drooping, I went into the house and made my lunch, a turkey and cheese sandwich, a peach, and a slice of chocolate cake. At least I wasn't eating a granola bar and a bruised apple, I thought, thinking back to Crystal and her scramble to stuff something into her stomach before her next appointment. I looked out the window as I savored slow bites of my dessert and gazed at the wide canopies of the catalpas arching over the entrance to my farm, their heart-shaped leaves fluttering in the light wind.

I set down my fork. I loved it here, and I *would* make this work no matter how much effort it took or what I had to give up.

No one and nothing was going to drive me away. Not without a fight. Not new arena lights, not lamed horses, not difficult boarders, not intrigue and undercurrents, not a terrible accident. At that last part, I gave a little shiver, but I suppressed it, set my dishes firmly in the sink, and started back out to begin my afternoon tasks.

Chapter Fifteen

With four days left until the Keystone Horse Exhibition Special opening ceremonies, tensions were rising at Catalpa Farm. Jessica and Marcy schooled their horses with fervor, and even Jason seemed to be lengthening his rides on Mayhem, although he kept to his evening schedule.

I began watching out the window for when he would arrive so I could meander out to the barn and keep a quiet eye on things. But Jason did nothing suspicious. He came and went without saying a word to me, doing his training rides with his usual quiet competence.

His demeanor around his horse was astounding, given how he acted around people. It made me shake my head. It also made me happy that for the most part, our paths were not crossing. I'd had no unpleasant interludes since the sign disagreement, and never received the promised email asking to have Mayhem moved to a stall without kick pads.

Valentina Hirsch came by in the afternoons to watch Jessica riding Goldrush and Midnight, then left after calling out instructions to Jessica, who often looked recalcitrant when I passed her in the aisle. I heard her complaining to Marcy about one of the directions

Valentina had left, and I had the feeling Jessica and Valentina's relationship was becoming strained.

Jessica was a skilled rider and trainer, and I thought she was doing a remarkable job with Midnight and Goldrush. Yet Valentina would stand and watch for the entire training session, dressed for riding in breeches and boots, a pair of gloves in her back pocket, just as if she were planning to climb on once Jessica finished. She never did. Instead, she stood, arms crossed on the top rail of the arena, observing and commenting and criticizing, and when the session was over, she roared away in her Porsche, music blaring. It would have driven me mad if I were Jessica and I was very glad I wasn't.

Marcy approached me one afternoon just as I was finishing with Donagin. She saw me gazing at Jessica and Midnight and raised her brows. "Jessica's quite a pleasure to watch, isn't she? She's got those two horses tuned up perfectly. Valentina should have no problem in the ring."

I looked at Marcy in astonishment. "*Valentina* is taking Goldrush and Midnight in the show? But ..." I hesitated. "I've never even seen her ride!"

Marcy laughed. "She's a decent rider. Nothing like Jessica, of course, but she'll get by."

I scrunched up my face. "It seems sort of odd, though," I began, and then stopped. Probably no point in broadcasting my ignorance.

Marcy shrugged. "It's not all that unusual in show circles. There are different classes for amateur owners, for professionals, and so on. If you've got the money, you can pretty much do anything you want. Lots of people use trainers."

"But, like, don't they also ride themselves? At least occasionally?"

"Yes." Marcy laughed. "Valentina's quite a character. Frankly, although she would never admit it, it doesn't help her in the show ring to be climbing on an unfamiliar horse. Although I'm guessing in the next day or two she'll pop in for a few rounds." Marcy paused and gestured toward the woods. "Hey, any chance that back trail will open up soon so we can use the cross-country paths?" I had been walking Donagin and she followed me as I led him toward the barn.

I put the horse in his stall, removed his halter, and hung it and the lead rope on their pegs. "I'm sorry," I said. "I didn't know anyone was interested in cross-country schooling, or I would have dealt with it. I'm not sure when the back trail will be open, but I could have broken a new path if I'd known. And built a jump or two."

Marcy shook her head. "I don't care about schooling over the jumps. It's just so pretty back there, and a nice way to cool the horses out after their work if we can walk through the woods."

"I understand," I said. "Let me look into it."

"I wouldn't mind giving you a hand, if that would be helpful," Marcy added, and I looked at her in surprise.

"Really? I don't want to take advantage."

"Not at all," Marcy said. "I'd be happy to do it."

Esther, after Crystal's skillful work on her abscess, was no longer lame. Another reason to get the new trail open was so I could finally get her out for one of the quiet rides I enjoyed so much.

"Okay. Maybe we could tackle that tomorrow morning?"

"Deal," Marcy said. She took a quick glance around the barn to see if anyone was listening. "Have you heard from J. D. Williams?" she asked in a low voice.

"Not a word," I said.

"But what did he say after he toured the barn?"

"He hasn't toured the barn. I wondered if he might contact me, but he hasn't."

"Jessica said—" Marcy broke off, looking confused and annoyed.

"What did Jessica say?"

Marcy sighed. "That he'd been through the barn and told Valentina he liked it, and he was considering Catalpa for one of his dressage horses when the dressage show opens."

"He hasn't toured the barn," I repeated. "Not with me, anyway. And no one should be taking him through the barn without permission." I felt a flash of anger, wondering if Valentina had deliberately brought him around when I wasn't present.

Do I need to put up security cams or something? I thought. I couldn't be here 24/7.

Marcy shrugged. "Well, if it's his dressage horses he wants to bring here, it won't affect me. The jumping part of the show will be over, and Songster'll be going home."

I didn't answer. I was still irate and concerned about the possibility that J. D. had come to the farm without my knowledge. If he had been at Catalpa, he'd come without permission, and if someone had taken him around the barns, they'd made a serious error. I didn't know who was in the stable at all times, but I did know what vehicles were in the lot, and I hadn't seen any unfamiliar cars. I supposed Valentina could have driven him in—there was no rule against guests—but if he had been here asking for a tour, she should have alerted me.

Of course, Marcy's information might be wrong, or Jessica's information might be wrong. And if he had been here, Valentina might not have brought him or shown him around. He might have walked over on his own—it seemed as if he'd been preparing to do that the other day. But something didn't smell right, and I didn't like it.

Cameron had moot court that evening, a simulated court proceeding that would help prepare him for his career in contract law. He'd been writing and preparing arguments all semester, and he wouldn't be back until very late.

So, it was in a sullen frame of mind—with the J. D. Williams conundrum hovering in my brain—that I stomped out to the barn after my solitary supper to finish up the chores and give my equine charges an evening flake of hay.

Jason's car was in the drive, but I didn't see Mayhem in the arena, so I figured Jason must have finished his evening ride. I hoped he wasn't just beginning, as it would be dark soon, and since I'd not yet come up with a solution for arena lights, he shouldn't be planning to start a round of jumping. I didn't relish a confrontation with him, but I should make sure I knew what his plans were.

It was with some surprise that I found the tack room was empty. Neither was he by AllBeCalm's stall. I stood in the aisle, scratching my head and wondering where he'd gone.

I decided to walk quietly over to the other aisle and see if he might be there. I hadn't meant to sneak around, but I was still in a bad mood, and after my suspicions that uninvited guests were taking advantage of the open nature of Catalpa's barns, I was feeling mistrustful and protective of my farm.

I slid the door to the second aisle carefully open just enough to peek in, and there was Jason in the growing shadows, standing with his back to me in front of Donagin's stall.

I had a momentary flash of alarm, but then I realized he had probably just stopped by there to see the horse. He was running his hands down Donagin's patient face and he held something out in his open palm. Donagin lipped it politely up and Jason was reaching into his pocket again when I decided to back quickly out of the doorway.

There was nothing nefarious about what Jason was doing unless he was poisoning Donagin, which I was certain he was not. I didn't want him to think I'd been spying on him when, of course, that was exactly what I'd been doing. I dreaded the confrontation if he suspected that. It made my brain hurt.

I hesitated outside in the waning sunlight, telling myself that if I harbored enough misgivings about Jason that I felt compelled to follow him around, I really should ask him to leave. It wasn't as if I hadn't been given ample cause. But yet, but yet ... what had he done, aside from being unpardonably rude? Elsa was positive he was the one who was threatening her, but was she right? What if she *was* right? Then what?

With these contradictory and confusing thoughts jumbling and rebounding around in my head, I slid the door the rest of the way open and walked nonchalantly in, just as if I were making my end-of-day rounds, which I was. The horses in this aisle still needed their evening snack, and I was going to give it to them, Jason or no Jason.

"Hey, Jason," I said offhandedly, pausing to peek into Paladin's stall and check his waterer.

Donagin was resting his muzzle in Jason's open palm, but at the sound of my feet coming up the aisle,

Jason pulled his hand back and turned to face me.

He scowled, customary for him, as I walked up.

"Nice evening," I commented, peeking into Donagin's stall and throwing in a flake of hay from the bale in the aisle.

Jason grunted.

"Did you have a good ride?" I asked.

"Yeah, fine. How long is this horse going to be on stall rest?"

I raised my brows. "The vet said six months. With controlled exercise, increasing very slowly."

"Looks like he's holding some swelling in that ankle," he commented, and turned to look at me, his dark eyes so cold it chilled me. Was I really standing here alone in my barn with this angry man? I took a step backward.

Jason's brows lowered in a scowl, and then he turned and strode away.

"The vet's monitoring him closely," I called after Jason, but he didn't acknowledge that he'd heard me. He just stalked out the door and soon disappeared toward the parking lot.

It was my turn to scowl, which I'd been doing a lot in the last few days. I couldn't decide whether to be relieved or insulted. I peeked at Donagin's ankle, looked over my shoulder to where Jason had disappeared, and shook my head. I stood stroking Donagin for a long time, then turned out the barn lights and made my way back up to the house, annoyed and unhappy.

I wished Elsa hadn't told me about the calls and letters. Or rather, I wished Jason's name hadn't come up as a suspect. I was uneasy about him and about his presence in my barn, and I didn't know what to do about it.

Chapter Sixteen

The next morning, I lingered over my coffee with Cameron in the DZ, sharing my worries about Jason Barlowe.

Cameron furrowed his brow and watched the steam rise from his cup into the cool morning air. "It's a challenge, that's for sure. It doesn't seem as if Elsa has any evidence that Jason's behind those threats, although it's suspicious."

I nodded and frowned. "Something about all this is bugging me."

"Yet he's never caused problems for you," Cameron pointed out.

"Besides being a rude pig," I said sourly.

"Besides being a rude pig," Cameron echoed. "How much longer will he be here?"

"He's paid up until the hunter section of the KHE Mayhem's in is over. Then maybe he'll be out of my hair. He'll either leave or pay for another month of board." We sat in silence for several minutes, sipping our coffee and gazing at the Catalpa barn, glowing gently in the early sunlight. "I suppose I should turn the horses out," I added. "I'm going to work on an alternate cross-country trail today. Marcy asked me about it and said she'd like to help."

"Where're you going to put it?"

"There's a stand of tulip poplars a little bit south of where the ramp was … is. I'm going to cut through there. It isn't quite as wooded as the other way, but it'll do for now. And if people like it, who knows? Maybe I'll maintain two paths."

"Was Joe Beers doing cross-country at KHE?" Cameron asked.

I furrowed my brow at what seemed to be an abrupt change of subject. "Not at the Special. There is no cross-country division. They'd need a way larger plot of land for a first-class cross-country course. There won't be any cross-country competition at KHE until the smaller shows later in the year."

"Why do you suppose Joe was out doing the cross-country jumps, then?"

"No idea," I said. "Just enjoying it, I guess. Like Marcy wants to do."

Cameron raised his brows. "Whoever killed Joe knew about him and his habits, it seems to me. Someone must have known him well. Did Jason?"

Aha. So, my husband was trying to figure out whether I was harboring a murderer in my barn. Delightful.

"Well, Jason definitely knew him. Joe was selling him AllBeCalm," I said. "Jason and Joe were my first two boarders, with Marcy and Songster close behind. He would have seen him out on the cross-country course. Joe was out there nearly every day."

"Hmm." Cameron shook his head. "We know Jason wasn't at Catalpa the day Joe was killed, but it would be child's play to get onto our property from the

KHE. Anyone could've gone there and walked over. It could have been Jason, but not just Jason. I know you suspect him, though, and he's sure not covering himself with positive regard."

I made a grab for my hair, planning to follow Cameron's lead and give it a good yank, but when Cameron glanced at my hand and grinned, I let go and sat back, smiling reluctantly. "Okay, enough of this. I need to go get started on my day. Thanks for confusing me."

Cameron sighed and leaned back. "My pleasure. You should have seen me in moot court. No one knew what to make of my arguments."

"Is that a good thing or a bad thing?" I asked cautiously.

"Oh, I knocked their socks off," Cameron said. "Sock-knocking is a very important talent."

I laughed. "Ooh, will you represent me when I'm declaring bankruptcy, Mr. Lawyer Man?" I asked, setting down my coffee cup and clasping my hands at my chest.

"Absolutely yes. I plan to only choose the cute clients," he said.

"Ha!" I glanced down at my torn jeans. "I better change, then. I'm dressed for trailblazing, not for cuteness."

"You're always cute. Take my word for it." He reached out and ruffled my short brown hair. "Cute, but tough."

I stuck my arm out and flexed my bicep, which Cameron obligingly pinched. "Wow!" he exclaimed, widening his eyes, and I gave him a playful punch. He stood and held out his hand. "Done with your cup?"

"Sure." I passed him my empty mug, and we went our separate ways. Cameron headed for the kitchen, and I headed for the stable.

Marcy arrived mid-morning, and I gave her a pair of work gloves to wear, along with some hedge shears. "You sure you don't want to ride first, Marcy?"

She shook her head. "I'd like to use the new trail for Songster and me to relax and cool out. Let's see how much we can get done."

"Okay then!" I smiled at her, and we loaded a shovel, a small electric saw, a bag of gravel, and a rubbish bin into the back of the side-by-side. Then we climbed in ourselves and headed out. It was a nice morning but on the cool side. Perfect for a day of cutting and digging.

We angled off the main trail into the woods, aiming at the tulip poplars, and found we could make good progress with the two of us working. We wound the trail through the trees, cutting away branches and brush and loading it in the back of the side-by-side, throwing some of the bigger stuff off into the woods, and filling in anything that looked like a low area in the path. We were fortunate that it appeared there was an old trail already cut through part of the woods, probably a deer trail. We just had to clear debris out of the way and make it wide enough for horses to travel.

I warned Marcy that she should only be walking the new trail for the first few days. No galloping until I could bring the roller out and tamp it all down. That had to wait until the dirt had settled a little.

I was surprised to see that we were nearly in line with the ramp after only about an hour and a half of work, thanks to the partial path that was already there. I was just checking my watch and wondering if I might squeeze in a quick ride on Esther before evening chores when I felt Marcy clutch my shoulder.

"Who's that?!" she asked.

I looked up. "Who's who?

"I just saw someone walking along the east trail," Marcy said in a loud whisper.

"Walking along the ... where?" I asked, and I looked where Marcy was pointing.

The spot where we had parked the side-by-side was densely overgrown, and it was hard to see out to the main trail, but I could just discern a figure striding along, heading with purpose toward Catalpa.

"What the—?" I snapped. "Not again!" I fired up the side-by-side, Marcy jumped in, and I wheeled it out to the trail we had just forged through the trees. "I do *not* want people coming across these trails from the KHE. What is the matter with everyone?" *And why haven't I put those signs up along the fence?* I scolded myself.

We had been speeding along for about fifty feet when suddenly Marcy gasped, "I know who that is! Stop! Stop!" and I had hardly slowed the vehicle when she leaped from the passenger seat and headed into the woods.

"Marcy!" I cried, looking over my shoulder, afraid she had injured herself, but there she was, standing among the trees, arms crossed and her face a mask of unhappiness.

And, of course, then I knew who it was. I didn't need to see the bright blonde hair and the chiseled, movie star face to know who was trespassing on Catalpa's property. It was J. D. Williams.

I motored out onto the main trail, ramming through brush and undergrowth in the as-yet uncleared part of the path. Then I charged up to him in the side-by-side, slamming it to a halt. He had stopped when he saw me coming and stood grinning widely. He pointed a playful finger at me when I climbed out of the vehicle and stalked up to him.

"Caught me!" he said in a singsong voice.

"This is private property," I said coldly. "You were asked to come around to the main gate."

"I know, I know!" he smiled a white-toothed smile. "But I like walking, and this is a lot nicer. You don't really mind if I come through here, do you?"

"Actually, I do. There's a cross-country trail here, and as I know you know, we had an accident recently. I need to know who is on my property and why. Please do as I asked. I would be happy to meet you up at the office and talk about whatever you came here to say."

I imagined I could hear Marcy saying *no, no, no, no*, although she was much too far away to hear our conversation.

J. D. shrugged and his face hardened a little. It wasn't an attractive look. "An accident," he scoffed. "If Joe Beers hadn't been such a fool, he wouldn't have been doing the cross-country to begin with. Everyone knew he liked to come out here and jump, and he never could control his horse. Besides, I heard there's some question about whether it was actually an accident."

I was so furious I had to clench my fists to keep my hands from shaking. It was remarkable how calm my voice sounded when I finally spoke, since in my brain was whirling the words, *Did you know he was out here, J. D.? And were you possibly also here on that day? What do you know about what happened?* "Joe was a fine rider," I said, dangerously quiet. "I'd be careful what you say."

Another look crossed J. D.'s face that was less easy to interpret. Fear? Dismay? I didn't know him well enough to distinguish. I wished Marcy were here with me so I could ask her, but she'd either hot-footed it back to the Catalpa barn or was still concealing herself in the tulip poplars.

There was a stony silence. Then J. D. turned on his heel and walked in the direction of the fence line. I stayed where I was and watched him go, debating whether I should follow and be sure he returned to the KHE grounds, but it felt awkward, so I decided against it.

Instead, I turned the side-by-side back around—awkwardly, since the path was narrow—and drove it back to where I'd left Marcy. She was still there, looking embarrassed and a bit guilty.

"I should've gone with you," she muttered.

"It's fine. I'm glad you stayed here to keep an eye on things."

Marcy frowned. "I nearly went back to the stable. But I wanted to be sure J. D. didn't ... well ... do anything. I don't trust him at all."

My heart gave a little lurch. "Is he violent, Marcy?"

She was silent for a long moment. "I've seen him shove his groom around. He never hit me or anything, but he's—um—not a nice guy. Don't be fooled by his good looks."

"Don't worry about that," I said firmly. In fact, my encounter with J. D. had made his good looks transform into something less than good-looking in my mind. He looked like a creep. I sighed. "This wasn't how I expected to spend our time out here. Shall we go back?"

Marcy looked around. "No, let's finish up. We're almost out to the main path, and with the trail you just broke with the side-by-side, a lot of our work is done!"

I smiled at her. One of the bad things about people cycling in and out as the KHE events came and went was that I'd make friends and then they'd move on. Marcy was one such. I'd miss her when she went back to Darrell Manning's home farm.

Chapter Seventeen

"You're going to like this news," Cameron said, striding into the living room and tossing an armful of books on the couch.

"What?" I looked up from my desk where I was once again buried in a pile of paperwork and bills. I glared at the mess. "Anything's got to be better than this."

Cameron walked over and kneaded my tight shoulders, then dropped a kiss on my head. "I ran into a police officer today, someone on the local force."

I looked up at him. "I don't get it."

Cameron grinned. "His name's Dennis Perry. Super nice guy. I see him quite often at the coffee shop and we like to sit and yak. He likes the same latte I get and we take turns buying. I knew he was with law enforcement, but I thought he was retired. Nope."

"Okay," I said slowly.

"We got to talking today," Cameron went on. "I already told him about Catalpa, and he knew about Joe's death. Anyway, I told him we were frustrated about not knowing when the trail could open, and he was sympathetic. He knows some of the ins and outs of the Joe Beers investigation. There's stuff he can't share, of course, but maybe he can at least give us an idea of when they'll remove the restrictions on the north trail. He said to call him if we have questions."

"Okay, that's super helpful," I said. "Marcy and I cut a new path today through the tulip poplars. I'd like to drag in a log or two eventually so there are some low jumps, but it's going to end up being a nice addition to the cross-country. I rode Esther through there late this afternoon as an experiment, and it worked out great."

"You rode Esther? That's good to hear."

"Yep. Crystal gave me the all-clear, and I think getting her to move around a little more will be good. I'll keep the protective boot on her for a while still, but we're making progress." Cameron and I fist-bumped. "Today wasn't perfect, though," I went on. "I ran into Mr. Good-Looking tramping uninvited through our property. Again."

"Mr. Good-Looking? Not that bozo from the KHE with the … what are they?"

"Trakehners. German horses." I never gave up trying to raise my husband's horse comprehension.

"Right, Trakehners." He mispronounced it, but I let it go. "The one who harassed Marcy?"

I nodded. "That's the one. Caught him walking where he'd been explicitly told not to. And I think he's done it before. Marcy has the impression he's been through the stables at some point."

"Was he? And why is he so obsessed with wandering around over here?"

"I have no idea. I didn't take him on any sort of tour of the grounds. If he did it at all, he came through alone or with one of the other people here. There's something I don't like about him, Cameron. He's super attractive, obviously, but he's smarmy or something." I tossed my pen onto the desk. "Plus, he admitted he knew Joe Beers was out on the cross-country jumps a lot. Said he was a fool and couldn't ride well enough to control his horse." I snorted. "As if Donagin is hard to control. Donagin's a complete gentleman. And even if he weren't, Joe was an accomplished rider, not a fool."

"Wait, he knew about Joe using the cross-country trail? Doesn't it seem as if he might be a suspect in—" Cameron broke off as my phone began stridently to ring.

I picked it up off my desk and clicked to answer. "Annie Parnell."

"Annie?" I looked at the display. The voice sounded familiar, but it wasn't a number I recognized.

"Yes, Annie Parnell," I repeated. "Who is this?"

"Jason Barlowe." I gave Cameron a wide-eyed glance and waited. "Look, I'm going to be—ah—detained for a while. I won't be able to get out there to ride. I need AllBeCalm to get some exercise or he'll ... He can be a difficult horse," Jason finished.

A difficult horse, I thought wryly. *That's an understatement.* However, to give Jason credit, once Mayhem had gotten into a steady riding schedule, his misbehaviors had decreased dramatically. I'd even wondered if the kick pads had been an unnecessary expense.

"Detained?" I asked cautiously.

"Yes, for a few days anyway." Jason's British accent was clipped and impatient. "If you could ... I'll pay you to get him some extra work."

I was tempted to say, *With what money?* but that wasn't fair. Jason had paid me for his stall space. He had no idea I knew about his financial difficulties. And I was rehabbing Donagin. Why not another horse? I sighed. Catalpa was becoming a stable of convalescents and cast-offs.

"I can do that," I said, trying to sound less reluctant than I felt. "A few days, you said?"

"Yes! I said a few days!" Jason responded angrily. "I've got to go." The line went dead. *There he is,* I thought. *There's the Jason I know and don't love.*

Cameron was staring at me curiously. "What was that all about?"

I shook my head and stared down at my phone. "That was Jason Barlowe. He asked—" and my phone rang again. This time I recognized the number.

"Hello, Elsa," I said.

"Annie!" Elsa's voice was shrill and I pulled the phone away from my ear, tapping speaker so Cameron could listen in. "I wanted to let you know right away, Jason Barlowe's been arrested!"

"Arrested?" I echoed, exchanging glances with Cameron, who put his arms out in a *What is going on around here?* gesture.

"Yes, arrested. Just a little while ago. I told the police about the calls and letter, and in the meantime, they did some analysis on that rope you found. You know, out in the woods?"

I grimaced. "Yes, I know the one." *How could I forget?* I thought but didn't say.

"Well, it's Jason's," Elsa said triumphantly. "It belongs to him and it's got his—I don't know—fingerprints or DNA or something on it. *And* he's got no alibi for the time when Joe was killed. I've been suspicious of him all along, and now they've got proof. I'm relieved and sad both at once, you know?"

"Yes, I can imagine," I replied, staring into Cameron's eyes. I'd had a murderer on my farm all this time? It was chilling.

"I think he killed him because he owed Joe the

money for that horse he has. AllBeCalm," Elsa chattered on. "It's a lot, you know, and he couldn't pay." I glanced at Cameron, and he gave a negative shake of his head. *Killing Joe wouldn't get him off the hook*, he mouthed. I held up a finger. Elsa was talking again. "The police tried to trace the calls, but they came from one of those throwaway phones. No fingerprints on the letter, either. But I know it was Jason. He's just … he's just …" Elsa apparently couldn't think of any insults awful enough because her voice trailed off.

"So, was he arrested for murder?" I asked, glancing at Cameron.

"No, not yet anyway." Elsa sounded triumphant. "The police went to talk to him about the threatening calls and the letter, and he got in a fight with them."

"A fight?" I echoed.

"Well, maybe not a fight. But he tried to punch one of them, so they arrested him."

There was a short silence while I digested that. *Good going, Jason. Take a swing at a cop. Always a smart move.* Then, "Thanks for letting me know," I said. "I'll need to deal with his horse."

"It's not his horse," Elsa said quickly, and I made a face.

"Right. I guess that's to be sorted out later?"

"Yes. I'll probably sell him once I get him back, but I've got too much to deal with right now. Can you just …?"

"Of course," I said. I wasn't going to tell her that Jason had already asked me to care for Mayhem. The situation was getting far too complicated. I sighed.

"I better go," Elsa said. "I'm sort of all in a dither. The autopsy results came back, and now I've got to plan Joe's m-memorial and all that. They're sh-shipping him home." I heard her voice falter. "He broke his neck. He was always so c-c-careful. But his vest wouldn't protect ... Annie, I'm going to let you go. I just called so you'd know what was going on."

"I appreciate it. Keep me posted."

"I will," Elsa replied, and we clicked off. I looked at my husband, eyebrows raised.

"Elsa seems to have made you her best friend," Cameron commented.

"Yes, she calls me kind of a lot," I said. "Not without reason though, usually. She's how I know as much as I do know about the investigation. Elsa cares about what happened to Joe and not so much about the impact it's having on me here, which is understandable, but it's nice to get at least some information. She said the autopsy's back. Maybe that means we can open the trail?"

"We should call the police tomorrow and ask."

"I will," I sat at my desk staring into space, then said. "Jason was arrested for the phone calls, but not for Joe's death?"

"Something about this doesn't seem right," Cameron said. "Things don't add up."

I sighed again. "I agree."

Chapter Eighteen

I found myself counting down the hours as the KHE approached and had inexplicable attacks of nerves, just as if I were in the show myself. I puttered around the barn making sure the feed was all organized properly, fussed over the vitamins and supplements each horse needed, called and hounded the company that delivered sawdust bedding to have them send it over early, and even did a deep clean of Esther's tack, although no one would see it except me.

And then there was Mayhem, who was as impatient with me as Jason was, and had taken to kicking the wall again. I lunged him as best I could while he bucked and threw himself around on the end of the long line Jason had left hanging on the stall, and I lifted my shoulders in a shrug when I returned him, prancing and nipping, to his paddock. I wasn't sure I was doing Jason any favors by exercising his horse for him. It didn't seem to be helping much.

There'd been no word whatsoever from Jason. I wondered what was happening, and wished for the fiftieth time that I had a way to get information from the police department. When I called and asked about re-opening the north trail, I received a firm *No* and *We'll be in touch.*

It rained all morning on T minus two days before the show opened, but although I was frantic that the arena was going to be too muddy to use and the riders wouldn't be able to practice, it held up just fine. There was one puddle in the corner that the horses had to dodge around, but other than that, we were hanging in there.

To relax, I took Esther out on a long amble on the cross-country trail, letting her walk along on a loose rein and enjoy the new path. I had an ulterior motive, too. I wanted to be sure no one from the KHE was wandering onto the property, especially J. D. Williams, but I didn't see anyone except Marcy, who seemed to be enjoying the trails as much as Esther and I were.

J. D. had never come by the office to inquire about stabling, as I had suggested. I gave a mental shrug. I didn't need him and his horses here anyway. I had new boarders coming in—I'd received two calls from people showing in the hunter division—and I *would* make ends meet this first year of Catalpa's existence.

In the early afternoon, I saddled Donagin and took him out to walk in the arena. I wanted to avoid Jessica and her training sessions under Valentina. Valentina had begun to grate on my nerves. She was so critical of Jessica, who I knew was a top-notch rider. I'd looked her up online one evening and found she'd been an accomplished competitor on her own before she'd joined up with Valentina. I suspected Valentina was paying her a bundle. You only had to look at the car Jessica drove to figure that out.

I looked down at Donagin's bobbing head as he patiently circled the arena and thought of Jason stopping by to see him the evening before he'd been arrested. That quiet scene had stuck in my mind for some reason.

Jason had a way with animals. My cats loved him. Mayhem would behave for only Jason, and Donagin ... I couldn't help but think back to that quiet moment I'd seen in the barn.

I pulled Donagin to a halt and sat up straight in the saddle, my eyes wide. All at once, I knew what had been bothering me about Jason and the accusations surrounding Joe's accident. Jason didn't like people, but would he kill someone? Probably his awful behavior was just bluster and bullying. I couldn't be 100% sure about that, but what I did know was that Jason would never hurt an animal.

Tripping Donagin had unseated Joe and caused him to have a fatal fall, but it could very well have been fatal for Donagin as well. It was extraordinarily fortunate for Donagin that he wasn't disastrously injured.

Jason understood horses. He would have known the perils to Donagin, had he done the horrible thing of stretching a rope across the trail in front of a galloping horse. He hadn't done it.

I sat on Joe's horse for a long time, wondering what to do. Call Officer Lopez? Call Cameron and ask him to find his friend at the law school coffee shop? I finished walking Donagin in something resembling a haze and was so distracted when I unsaddled him that I didn't hear Marcy come into the barn and call to me.

"Hello! Hey, Annie!" Marcy strode up, dressed in breeches and boots, ready for her session with Songster.

I jumped. "Marcy! I was completely in another world. What's up?"

"Nothing. I just came to say hi before I saddle up. We're in the last stretch, I guess! Darrell's coming in tomorrow afternoon so he can cheer on Songster at the show. He's staying at the East End B&B with his wife, but they hope to watch Songster school here at least once. I wanted to let you know."

"I appreciate it," I said. "I look forward to meeting him."

So, he wants to see his horse go, after all, I thought, and felt a little more kindly toward Mr. Manning.

Marcy smiled. "See you!" she added. "And by the way, we're loving the new cross-country trail. I'm very glad we took the time to do it."

"So am I." I smiled at her warmly as she left the barn and started for Songster's paddock.

Then I pulled my phone out of my pocket, hurried into the barn office adjoining the tack room where I could have some privacy, and dialed Cameron. I got his voicemail.

I decided to take the bull by the horns and call Officer Lopez, whose voicemail I also got. "Officer Lopez? This is Annie Parnell at Catalpa Farm. I wanted to talk to you about Jason Barlowe and Joe Beers' murder, in case he was … in case you were … Well, it's difficult to explain, sort of. Could you maybe call me?"

Well, great, Annie, I thought when I clicked off. *Incoherent much? Blather much?*

I sighed in frustration and set my phone down on Esther's saddle. If Officer Lopez called me back at all, and I wouldn't have blamed her if she didn't, would I be helping or hurting Jason's case? If I said I was positive Jason wouldn't hurt an animal and that was why he couldn't have killed Joe, I had the feeling that wasn't exactly going to sound sensible. Nor was it definitive of anything. He wouldn't hurt an animal, but would he hurt a person?

I wasn't even sure the police suspected him of

anything beyond being a hothead, which he was. Maybe all I had done was make things worse. And for some reason, I wanted to help him. I didn't want grumpy, rude, horrid Jason to be guilty of murder and I didn't think he was.

It was only then that I noticed I had a voicemail myself. My phone had been turned to silent while I rode Donagin, and I'd missed the call.

I checked my messages. The call was from Elsa, and she sounded upset, as she had been the last half dozen times I'd talked to her, except this time she was both upset and angry.

"Annie, I'm so sorry to bother you, but something's happened. Would you give me a call?"

I frowned. *Something's happened.* I didn't like the sound of that. I pressed dial and listened to the phone begin to ring on Elsa's end.

"Annie!" Elsa cried, not bothering with a greeting. "I need some help!"

"What's going on?" I asked, trying to keep my voice calm.

"I've been going through Joe's emails …" she hesitated. "I had to. I couldn't find the password to one of our accounts, and so I was looking … I wasn't snooping."

I interrupted her. "Elsa, I understand you're concerned about Joe's privacy, but you need to do what you need to do. You don't need to explain."

"I know, but …" She seemed to be struggling to speak. She went on so quietly that I had to press the phone to my ear. "I found all these messages from someone. Do you know anyone named Cuore?"

"Um, no. Not that I can think of."

"Someone in the horse show world

somewhere?"

"I don't know anyone by that name," I repeated. "But the horse world is pretty big, Elsa. I only know the people who have horses here, and maybe one at the show ... so far, that is." I thought of J. D. Williams over at the KHE and scowled.

"Maybe someone with a string of horses?"

"It still doesn't help, Elsa. It could be anyone. Have you tried Googling it? What is happening?"

There was a long silence. "He was having an affair, Annie."

"Who?"

"Joe!" Elsa exclaimed. "Joe was."

"An affair?" I was shocked. "You mean, like, recently?"

"Well, no." Elsa's voice strengthened. "It was before we married, but not that long before. The person was trying to talk Joe into giving them a horse. I think it might have been AllBeCalm, but I'm not sure. And it sounds as if maybe he was thinking about letting her—I guess it's a her—have the horse."

"Dumb question, but I presume the messages weren't signed?"

"Not the ones I've found so far. And it's a random Gmail account called *cuore*."

"That isn't necessarily a person's name. It could mean almost anything."

"I know. I'm so frustrated, Annie, I just can't tell you."

"Could the messages be from Jason?"

Elsa cleared her throat. "No. They aren't from Jason. They're steamy. Racy. Rated X, even."

I raised my brows. Steamy, racy emails between Jason and Joe would certainly put a different spin on things. But, no. I agreed with Elsa. Jason wasn't *cuore*.

"Do you think this means anything about Jason's case?" I finally asked cautiously.

"I have no idea." Now Elsa sounded angry. "I'm tired of all this. I'm very upset, Annie. An affair like that, right before we married? I don't know what to think. And I don't want to look up anything else on his computer. I don't know what I'm going to find, and at this point whatever it is I'm probably not going to like it."

"I can understand that," I said gently. "Maybe set it all aside for a while? Do you need the password right now?"

"No, I suppose not. You're right. I'm going to shut the computer down. All this is doing is upsetting me."

"I hear you," I said soothingly.

"But if you come across anyone named Cuore, would you let me know?"

I smiled to myself. She was letting it go for now, but not really. "Yes, I will," I said.

We clicked off and I sat staring at the neat row of bridles hanging on the wall in the tack room. If someone else felt they were entitled to AllBeCalm, for whatever reason, and Jason knew about it, wasn't that a reason to threaten Elsa not to reclaim him?

Maybe it was a good thing I hadn't reached Officer Lopez after all.

Chapter Nineteen

"I phoned Dennis Perry," Cameron told me. "I didn't see him at the coffee shop today, but I think he's around. I had to leave a voicemail, though." And just then his phone rang.

I'd told my husband about the call from Elsa, and about the other happenings of the day—mainly the new trespass by J. D. Williams, and he had been staring moodily off toward the barn, his wine untouched.

Now he grabbed his phone, looked at me and said, "It's Dennis." Then he clicked to answer. "Hi, Dennis. Thanks for calling back ... Oh, okay. Thanks. We were wondering because, as I think I told you, he's got a horse here, and my wife is taking care of it while he's—um—unavailable." Cameron made a face at me. Then, "Really? ... That's interesting ..." There was a long silence while Cameron listened. I caught his eye and he mouthed, *Sorry. But this is important.* Then, "Yes ... Thanks for that, it helps," he said, and he signed off.

"What?" I asked, wishing he'd had the phone on speaker.

"Jason's being released. He's out on bail from the scuffle with the police, and he's not being charged for those calls to Elsa."

"Wow," I said.

"He's also not being charged for anything to do with Joe's death. I mentioned to Dennis in one of our coffee shop meets that we were concerned about that. He just told me Jason's got an alibi for when Joe was killed. He was at his kid's soccer game."

I raised my eyebrows.

"Yeah, I know," Cameron said. "Dennis was oversharing, but he understands what we're dealing with. And he knows I'm trustworthy."

"Jason was at a *kids'* soccer game?" It sounded so incongruous I nearly laughed.

Cameron shrugged and nodded. "Turns out Jason's divorced from his wife, but she lives in this area with their daughter, who plays soccer. He goes and watches the games from a distance when he's here for shows at the KHE. Usually sneaks in and stays incognito because of some unpleasantness. I'm not sure of the details."

"Jason lives in Illinois now," I put in. "Quite a hike to see his daughter. No wonder he wants to see her while he's here showing."

Cameron shrugged. "Apparently, no one remembered seeing him at the game at first, and his ex-wife claimed he wasn't there, but then a former neighbor remembered that he'd been standing at the edge of the parking lot watching and spoke up."

"Well, that's good for Jason," I said.

"The problem is," Cameron went on. "The rope that was used belonged to Jason. He freely admits that. It's even got a tag with his initials on it. And his DNA is all over it. There were horse hairs and blood, too, but no clear evidence that anyone else had handled it."

"Elsa mentioned that," I said.

Cameron frowned. "I suppose the murderer could have worn gloves."

"Well, everyone wears them who works around horses, or who rides. I have about ten pairs."

"True."

"And how did the murderer get hold of the rope?"

"No idea. Something the police are going to have to figure out. But he's got a solid alibi for when Joe was killed. He's off the suspect list. Let's keep this to ourselves. I'm sure Dennis told me far more than he should have, but it's comforting, anyway, to know Jason isn't a murderer."

I shuddered. *Murderer*. So, Jason probably hadn't killed Joe, but someone had. Was it someone else here at Catalpa? It was a frightening thought. It was one thing to be suspicious of Jason, but now it seemed everyone was a suspect. I paced up and down the living room. The light rain had resumed, so the DZ was off-limits. "I have some news, too," I said. I told Cameron about Elsa's call and how I'd been going back and forth about Jason's innocence.

"Cuore." Cameron rubbed his chin. "Why does that sound familiar to me?"

"It *does*?" I asked. "Elsa wondered if it was someone on the show circuit, but I don't know anyone named that. Of course, I don't know much of anyone showing at KHE. Besides, it might not be anyone's name at all. It could mean anything, or mean nothing, and someone just made it up for an email ID."

"I'm going to do an Internet search," Cameron said. He got up from the table and walked into the bedroom. "See if I can find someone named that who shows horses. I still say it sounds familiar."

"Go for it," I said. "I've got chores to do. I wonder when Jason'll be back out. I'd be AOK with turning Mayhem back over to him any old time."

I went out to the barn and started my usual tucking-in ritual. Checking horses, giving them all a bite of hay for the night, checking gates and the tack room door. I looked thoughtfully at the latch on the tack room, wondering if I should install a lock on it. Maybe one of those touchpad ones with numbers that I'd give to the people stabling horses at Catalpa. There was a lot of high-end equipment here, and my trio of cats wasn't going to be much use in the security department.

Ron wound around my ankles, purring and meowing for his evening snack. "If I lock this door," I informed him, "you and your buddies are going to need to have your food bowls somewhere else." Ron looked up at me, contemplating that, and I reached to scratch his head. "I'll make sure it's somewhere good, don't worry."

Ron didn't look convinced, but I ignored his skepticism and started again for the house. *I'll make it work. I will.* I repeated to myself, while at the same time pondering the cost of installing a locking system on my barn.

Chapter Twenty

One more day until the KHE Special opened. I still hadn't heard from Jason, and I wondered if I should work AllBeCalm. I decided to put it off for a little while in hopes that Jason would show up to work the manic animal. I put his horse out in the paddock and watched with a sigh as he bucked his way from one end to another, twisting and lunging and launching into the air. I hoped he wouldn't hurt himself before Jason had another crack at calming him down.

And would Jason be able to show him, or had too much time passed without Mayhem getting any real work?

I went back in the barn to saddle Esther for my daily ride and hack out along the trails, and there I ran into Marcy.

She grinned and gestured toward the paddocks. "I see AllBeCalm is getting his daily workout. That horse is incredibly athletic. Too bad he can't channel his energy into something a little more productive."

"Jason seems to be able to do that," I commented. "He rides him like he's no big deal. Maybe that's the secret. Not letting him think he's a big deal. I haven't mastered that strategy!"

"Could be. What's going on with Jason, anyway? Are they going to throw him in prison?"

"Not without a trial," I said quickly. "Besides, he's out, last I heard."

"Out?" Marcy looked surprised and a little alarmed.

"Out of jail. He was arrested because of his attitude with the police, but he's not being charged with anything to do with Joe's murder." I'd almost explained about Jason's daughter and his alibi, but I realized I'd be breaking confidence with Dennis Perry, so I held my tongue.

"Well, I'll be," Marcy said. "That'll be a big surprise to Jessica, and even more to Valentina. I think Valentina was a little worried about Jason and AllBeCalm riding against her horses, but also against J. D.'s group. I'm sure she didn't want him arrested, but it got him out of the way. If AllBeCalm's on his game, he's unstoppable. Neither Valentina nor Jessica will like it if he's back in the running. And neither will J. D."

"Well, I don't know if he is or not. Back in the running, that is. Jason asked me to work AllBeCalm for him, but he hasn't shown up and hasn't called. No contact at all. And the only schooling his horse has had in the last few days is me attempting to lunge him. Not very successfully, I fear."

Marcy raised her brows. "Jessica'll be out later. I better tell her."

"She'll find out soon enough," I pointed out.

"Yeah, but she'll need to tell Valentina so Valentina can tell J. D." She made a face and said J. D.'s name in a breathy whisper.

I grimaced.

"J. D. What a creep. I'm not sure what Valentina

sees in him," Marcy snapped. She continued toward Songster's paddock while I went to saddle Esther.

Later, as Esther and I were finished in the arena and heading out to circle the trails, I saw Marcy sitting on Songster, reins hanging loose, and texting on her phone. She caught my eye and nodded toward the cross-country. "Want some company?"

"Sure," I replied, and she trotted Songster over to catch up with me as we ambled down the lane.

Marcy looked around and sighed. "It sure is pretty here. I love your farm, Anna. I wish we could stay longer."

"Me too," I said. "The show hasn't even started and I'm already missing the people and horses that have been stabling here. Maybe not AllBeCalm," I added, and Marcy grinned.

"I told Jessica about Jason coming back," Marcy said. "She's going to pass the news on to Valentina. That'll be a nightmare, I'm sure."

"Poor Jessica," I said. "Will Valentina be angry at her?"

Marcy shrugged. "There's nothing to be angry about, really. And certainly nothing to blame Jessica for. Except she won't want her horses up against Jason and AllBeCalm in the show ring. She's very competitive, and J. D. is, too. They're a good match in that way, and of course anything J. D. wants is what Valentina wants, too." Marcy rolled her eyes.

"I hope Jason can still show AllBeCalm. The horse hasn't had any good schooling since I took over."

"Good point. But, if Jason scratches, that'll make Valentina very happy." Marcy grinned. "C'mon, let's trot. I adore these trails. Darrell's coming by in about an hour to watch Songster jump, so soon I need to stop indulging

myself and get to work."
 I smiled and pressed my heels to Esther's sides.

Chapter Twenty-One

Marcy and I put our horses away while Jessica worked Paladin and waited for Valentina to arrive. She took the flashy chestnut over jump after jump, all seemingly perfect in my eyes. Jessica apparently thought so, too, because she lavished praise on the horse as she walked him from the arena, casting a glance at the parking lot.

I wondered if she was hoping to get finished with Paladin before Valentina came. Jessica had wanted so badly to take Paladin in the Special. It was a shame she wasn't going to be able to do that.

Darrell Manning and his wife came and watched Songster and Marcy's lovely workout, Songster soaring over the jumps like a big gray bird. Marcy had mentioned AllBeCalm and Jason being unstoppable, but I thought Marcy and Songster could give them a run for their money. Then Marcy put Songster away, and the Mannings left to take Marcy out to a local restaurant.

I decided to use the quiet time before Valentina blew in to get some work done in the barn office, sorting through papers and making a pile for recycling. When Catalpa first opened, I'd done all the farm business here, but as time went on, I moved to the house office—partly because it was more convenient to be close to the printer and there were more file cabinets, and partly because it was lonely in the barn by myself. At least Cameron, his nose buried in his books, was in a nearby room. But that didn't mean I could let the barn office turn into a trash heap.

Later, I saw Jessica lead Goldrush out of the barn toward the arena for his schooling session. *Valentina is late today*, I thought idly. *If she doesn't come soon, MidnightInVerona's is the only ride she'll catch.* I wondered if she'd ride either horse today. If she planned to show them, now was certainly the time.

And then I heard her roar into the parking lot, music blaring, and her car crunched to a halt on the gravel. I watched out the window as she strode toward the stable, dressed in expensive riding gear as usual, slapping her gloves against her hand.

Sighing, I returned to my sorting and recycling and, looking up, noticed how dirty the globe was on the overhead light fixture. I abandoned the paper piles and dragged my office chair over. Then, with Cameron's imagined voice shouting in my head, *Don't stand on a rolling chair! Get the stepstool!* I climbed up, a rag in my hand, to swab away the worst of the dust. *I need to bring out some window cleaner to really do a good job*, I told myself. This had years of build-up on it. The light would be considerably better in the office once the globe was clean. Maybe I'd actually be able to see to work if I decided to move some of my operation back here.

And I should keep the office door closed, I thought. *This room picks up dust from everywhere.*

There were hoofbeats in the aisle—Jessica leading Goldrush back into the barn. With Valentina—an angry Valentina—in tow I realized. Their raised voices reached me where I stood on the chair in the office, and

I reached up to finish wiping off the light fixture before I climbed down.

Goldrush's stall door slid open. Jessica had led the horse inside.

"Well, you didn't answer your phone," I heard her snap. "I tried to call as soon as Marcy told me, but you were ... You were doing whatever."

Jessica's pronunciation of the word *whatever* implied something very disagreeable. I reached to swipe away one more cobweb and then froze, the dustcloth dangling, as I heard the next words.

"Besides," Jessica went on, her voice rising, "he should never have gone to jail to start with. I saw the rope, Valentina, remember? You said it was Joe's. It had his initials on it, and I believed you at first. But it wasn't Joe's, was it? It was Jason's."

J. B., I thought. *Jason Barlowe or Joe Beers.* They had the same initials, but it was Jason's DNA they'd found on the rope. I stiffened in my precarious position on the chair. A frightening suspicion had entered my head.

Valentina gave a tinkling laugh. "What're you sayin' honey? That lunge line was Joe's. Not much of a goin' away gift, was it?"

"It wasn't Joe's. You went to Catalpa and got it," Jessica said coldly. "I know you did. You walked over to Catalpa and grabbed Jason's lunge rope. And we didn't have that rope before."

"Jess, honey, you're bein' ridiculous. You're right that I went to Catalpa, but it was only to look at the accommodations." Another laugh. "I had to sneak in. Can you believe it? That stupid cow gets her dander up if anyone walks across her property, but half the time she doesn't even know who's here. She was ever so rude to J. D."

There was a crash and I jumped, grabbing the light fixture to keep my balance. It sounded as if Jessica had punched the wall. "We didn't have that lunge line before, Valentina," she repeated. "Don't you think I know our equipment? You came here and took it. But you shouldn't have left it over at the showgrounds with J. D.'s things. He saw it, too, and asked me about it. You took it, didn't you? To set up Jason Barlowe." Her voice was clipped, furious. And afraid? "Jason had the horse you wanted. Joe told you he might give him to you, and then you and Joe split up and he met Elsa."

"That's a serious accusation, Jess." Valentina's musical accent suddenly sounded threatening. "Be careful, now."

But Jessica went on, her voice hard. "When Jason was arrested, I thought I was imagining things, especially since you brought our horses here. That was a gutsy move, even for you."

I teetered on the chair, appalled at what I was hearing. I started to lower one foot down but froze when the chair creaked. I couldn't let them know I was overhearing their conversation. I glanced around the office. Could I climb down and find a place to hide?

"Well," I heard Valentina say indignantly, "I couldn't have our horses in those trashy stalls over at the showgrounds."

Jessica gasped. "You just think you can get away with anything, don't you? But you can't. I heard Jason wasn't anywhere near here when Joe died. But you were, weren't you? You stretched that rope across the trail and made Donagin fall. I suspected it all along."

"Jessica!" Valentina protested. "If Joe got hurt, it served him right."

"Served him *right*?" Jessica gasped. "Served him

right?"

"He owed me that horse," Valentina hissed, "and then he dumped me like a load of ... a load of manure. I just wanted to pay him back a little."

There was an appalled silence, then Jessica said, "I thought you'd deny it, I really did. But you killed him, didn't you? Was that how you paid him back?"

For a moment, Valentina's voice wavered. "Well, I didn't exactly—"

"He died, Valentina! He died!" Jessica interrupted. "You murdered him!"

"Jessica, honey, that's a terrible thing to say," Valentina purred. "But we're partners, right? You help me and I help you? How was I supposed to know he'd break his neck? He shouldn't have cheated me out of that horse or with that bitch he married. It was the only thing I could think of to get back at him, and you can't believe what a horrible time I had. First Joe falls and stupidly dies, then I couldn't get the rope untied and I had to leave it there. I nearly had hysterics!"

"You nearly had hysterics?" Jessica echoed shrilly. "There's a dead man, and you're upset about the rope?"

"I didn't want anyone to find it, obviously!" Valentina exclaimed. There was a short silence, then "Come here, honey," crooned Valentina. "You're overexcited. Once you think about it, you'll see it was the only thing to do."

"Get away from me!" Jessica barked. "Get away from me, Valentina!"

"'Get away from me?' You say that after all I've done for you? All I've given you?"

"You can't always bribe and manipulate people into doing what you want," Jessica snarled. "And I won't be a party to a crime! I'm done."

Jessica slammed into the tack room, Valentina grabbing at her arm. Then the two of them stood there, mouths agape, staring at me through the open office door as I stood wobbling on the rolling chair and gripping the light fixture, my heart slamming against my ribs. Then Jessica brushed past Valentina, snatched up her purse from the saddle rack, and ran. Her footsteps echoed down the barn aisle and out to the driveway.

"Well!" Valentina looked at me and shook her head, her dark curls dancing around her face. "That girl is a crazy one!" She gave another of her lilting laughs, but she was walking slowly toward me, and the look on her face wasn't laughing at all.

I didn't bother answering. I held onto the light fixture for dear life, my breath and my thoughts racing. I had the insane notion that perhaps I could use the globe to pull myself up to the ceiling and away from her, but it was my terror talking.

Valentina smiled. "You better come down from there, honey, before you hurt yourself. It's not safe standin' on that chair like you are." She reached out and gave the chair a shove. It rolled backward about a foot and I grabbed wildly at the light to steady myself. To my horror, one side of it started to come loose from its moorings, and a screw tumbled to the floor.

A flow of awful images flashed through my head. A broken arm, a broken shoulder, a broken hip, a broken head.

I clutched the back of the chair with one hand, hoping to get my leg down, but Valentina gave it another shove and I had to stand and grip the globe again to keep my balance. This time it came loose in my hands.

A broken back, I thought. And once I was down

on the floor, what would Valentina do? Maybe she wouldn't have to do anything. I imagined my head smashing against the floor and thought I might vomit. *I might never ride my Esther again,* my brain shrieked.

I didn't stop to think any further. Solely on impulse and with absolutely no expectation of success, I grasped the glass globe in both hands and threw it with all my might at Valentina's head. The chair skittered away and I grabbed wildly at the backrest, managing to keep my balance with a supreme act of will.

My aim was perfect. The globe hit Valentina like a missile, splintering and scattering across the floor. She crumpled under the blow with a loud cry, and I saw with a certain amount of malevolent satisfaction that as she fell, she put her hand on a sliver of broken glass, and blood began to seep out from between her fingers.

I leaped off the chair and dodged the shattered globe, stumbled, but then slipped clear of Valentina's hand, which she had thrust out in a vain effort to catch hold of my ankle. Then I sprinted away down the barn aisle, shrieking at the top of my lungs. "Help! Help!"

I burst out into the yard still yelling, and to my shock crashed straight into someone who had just come up the path from the parking lot.

He grabbed me by the shoulders to steady me and looked down at me, his dark face exasperated and confused. Jason Barlowe.

"What are you doing? What's going on?" he growled, his British accent clipped and angry. But this time it sounded like music in my ears.

"Help!" I croaked. "Valentina Hirsch …" I gasped and struggled to catch my breath, my fear like an icy wave down my back. For a moment, Jason stared at me in astonishment. Then his face hardened. He looked past me, pushed me roughly to one side, and strode toward the barn.

    I didn't wait to see what was going to happen. My heart still thundering in my chest, I stumbled toward the house. I paused as I reached the parking lot and, my breath tearing in my lungs, I dragged my phone out of my pocket to call 9-1-1.

    Jessica was nowhere in sight. Her BMW sat gleaming in the sun, beautiful and abandoned.

Chapter Twenty-Two

It turned out the DZ had more than one purpose.

Besides being our private discussion zone, it was also a calming, steadying place where I could share my worries and fears with my husband, relive awful experiences, and sit quietly holding his hand.

"She won't be able to dodge away from all of it, you know," Cameron said. "Jessica won't. She's an accessory, although it won't be like Valentina's crime. Not first-degree murder. I suppose what she is charged with will depend on how well she can convince the police that she had no real reason to suspect Valentina, especially with Jason Barlowe in the spotlight as the possible perp." He rubbed his chin.

I glowered at him. "Thinking of becoming a criminal attorney?"

Cameron grinned. "Not really. I just can't resist running through it in my head. You have to admit, criminal law could be more interesting than contracts."

I shivered. "It was awful, Cameron. If Jason hadn't come when he did, I don't know what would have happened."

"Sounds like he didn't have to do much," Cameron gave a small smile. "You beaned Valentina a good one. All Jason had to do was hold the tack room door closed until the police came."

"It was awful," I repeated. "I guess Valentina screamed and pounded and clawed to get out."

"I'm sorry, love." Cameron looked contrite. "I'm not making light of what happened at all. At *all*," he repeated firmly. "I owe Jason for stepping in and helping you. He's a formidable guy, and he kept his head, detaining Valentina like he did. I'm just going over it and wondering if anyone else was involved. J. D. Williams for one."

I shrugged. "I don't care what happens to J. D. Williams. He was an idiot for getting taken in by Valentina. I was heaping curses on him for walking across our property, and he was only doing what Valentina had already done. She probably talked him into it."

"Maybe she did," Cameron grimaced. "But you told him not to cross the property and he did anyway. Just speculating here, but … you said he's got gambling debts?"

"Crystal told me that, yes."

"What if he was hoping to blackmail Valentina? Maybe, like Jessica, he suspected what Valentina had done and hoped to find some evidence here?"

I stared at my husband. "Now that's an interesting thought. I kept wondering what he was doing and why he kept coming to Catalpa. Supposedly he and Valentina were a thing, but maybe he was taking advantage of her. Do you suppose we'll ever know?"

Cameron shrugged.

"I think it's a sure thing Valentina'll try to spread some of the blame to him," I mused. "He'll get mixed up in it no matter how hard he tries to wiggle out."

"I'm also wondering," Cameron looked up at the

ceiling, "whether Jason had some suspicions about Valentina. It sounds as if he didn't hesitate to protect you from her. Did he know she was dangerous? You ran out of the barn calling for help. How did he know you were running from her? Maybe you needed help because she'd injured herself. Or ... who knows what?"

"Well," I commented wryly, "if he did have suspicions, he should keep that to himself. He doesn't need any more problems with the police."

Cameron stared out at the quiet barn. "So, the only one left of our gang who is going to be in any classes at the KHE is Marcy. Jason had to drop out, and Valentina's not going to be showing her horses anytime soon—or ever."

I sighed. I feared Jessica wasn't going to be back in the show ring anytime soon, either. And I felt badly for Jason. AllBeCalm just wasn't ready to show after his forced layoff, so Jason had done the wise thing and scratched him. "At least for now," I told Cameron and gave a slight smile. "I've got four more people and seven horses coming in about a week, so Catalpa still has another chance at glory. And Marcy and Songster cleaned up yesterday afternoon."

"Nice for her," Cameron commented.

"*Really* nice, yes. I've enjoyed having her here. She'll be gone in a few days, but I expect she'll be back next year. She said she told Songster's owner, Darrell Manning, that this is a much better place to be than at the showgrounds."

"Yay, Marcy!" Cameron pumped his fist.

"I heard Valentina had to have ten stitches in her hand," I said. "Marcy told me." It was something of a *non sequitur*, but it gave me some malicious joy.

"Good," said Cameron, and I smiled at him.

I sighed. "Well, I guess it's time for evening chores," I said, pushing myself up out of my chair.

"Want some help tonight?"

"Why, sure," I said, and my phone rang. I picked it up and glanced at the display, then looked at Cameron. "Elsa Kurchner again. I wonder what this is about. I don't need any more drama right now."

"You better talk to her," Cameron said. "Let's get this over with."

I clicked to answer. "Hi, Elsa. How are you doing?"

Cameron leaned in, and we sat close together, the phone on speaker.

"I'm doing okay," she said. "I've got a memorial announcement for you to distribute. Could I email it to you?"

"Of course."

"Also, are you busy? I found out some things and wanted to talk to you about what I've decided."

"Well ..." I made a face and exchanged glances with Cameron. "Sure. Go ahead."

"First of all, I wanted to let you know who *Cuore* is."

"You figured it out?"

"I did. It actually wasn't all that hard."

"Who is it?" I asked.

"It's Valentina Hirsch," Elsa said unhappily. "One of my friends is Italian, and she recognized *cuore* as meaning heart. You know, heart, Valentine, Valentina? I'll bet you anything that's where she came up with that handle. But besides, she slipped in one or two emails, and I caught it. She was determined to get Joe back after he broke up with her, and she wanted AllBeCalm. She was obsessed with it. In the end, she was pressuring him hard—really hard, more like threats. You could tell he was trying to get rid of her. He even said he was going to block her if she didn't quit."

I shook my head. "She's ruthless, that's for sure. And obsessed with good horses."

"Later, I think she thought if I was convinced Jason was threatening me, maybe I'd take AllBeCalm back and sell him to her. She's completely nuts. By the way, I'm turning all those emails over to the police. Joe would be so embarrassed by them, but they need to know. I told you I was going to stop looking, but I couldn't help myself. And as it turns out, I'm glad I didn't stop, because there's more."

I sighed. I wasn't sure I wanted to know more. It was all distasteful and upsetting, and I just wanted it to be done.

"Hello?" Elsa said.

"I'm here." I didn't want to ask, but I did. "What else did you find?"

"In another email ..." Elsa went on, and I couldn't help squeezing my eyes shut. It seemed the list of Valentina's misdeeds was growing longer and longer. "In another email, or group of emails, I found correspondence between Jason Barlowe and Joe. I guess—and I know this sounds crazy—Jason and Joe were actually kind of friendly, or at least they understood each other, weird as it sounds."

"Wow," I said, and made a face at Cameron, wondering how anyone could understand Jason.

"Joe told Jason that he thought Jason and AllBeCalm suited each other in personality ..."

I smiled grimly. "I'd say that's quite true. Both of them are volatile and unpleasant." *But Jason might have saved my life,* I thought. Who knew what would have happened if he hadn't come along when he had?

"... And Joe said in the email that he wasn't going to be a stickler about the payments because he thought Jason and the horse belonged together. He wasn't sure he could find anyone else to take him if Jason wouldn't, and he wasn't going to let Valentina have him. He didn't say how the payments should happen, but I'm going to work something out with Jason because that's what Joe wanted. I feel terrible about Jason being arrested. I was responsible for him ending up in jail. I was so sure …" Elsa's voice trailed off. Then she said, "I completely overreacted and exaggerated a lot of things, and I'm very ashamed." She cleared her throat. "I don't even know why I said some of the things I did. Joe wasn't afraid of Jason. I actually think he was rather afraid of Valentina. I feel absolutely awful."

"'Hell hath no fury …'" Cameron murmured in my ear. I turned to look at him and nodded. Valentina was a woman scorned. A man had lost his life because of it.

"Valentina likes to collect horses," I said to Elsa. "She seems to attach herself to men with good horses and then she tries to wheedle-persuade-extort-whatever, the guy into something."

Elsa snorted. "Well, she didn't get away with it this time. I was furious at Joe for a while, but I guess I was wrong about that, too. Oh well." She sighed heavily.

I didn't answer. It seemed as if Joe and Elsa had been happy for the short time they'd had together. It would have been too bad for that memory to be spoiled. I hoped she could put the sordid parts of all this behind her and truly mourn her lost husband.

Elsa seemed to have run out of things to say. "It was good to talk to you, Elsa," I tried. "Cameron and I were just going to finish up the chores, so I'd better let you go. Email me that notice, and I'll make sure to send it around. I hope you can get some rest tonight."

I'll go shut down my computer, Cameron mouthed and started for his office.

"One more thing," Elsa spoke up.

"Okay." *What now?* I thought, my heart sinking. I just wanted this all to be over and for life to get back to normal. I wanted to have my beautiful farm and enjoy the horses, and—most of all—grab onto a few days of peace. Maybe have a date night with my husband. Maybe that live music we'd been talking about.

"Donagin," said Elsa.

"Yes," I said. "He's coming along well. I've been riding him and keeping an eye on him. Crystal Ellis, the vet, will ultrasound him again the end of this week."

"I'd like you to have him."

I felt my jaw hit the table. Cameron had turned back, and he and I stared at each other in astonishment. "What did you say?" I asked.

"I'd like you to have him," Elsa repeated. "I've got my hands full with a lot of things right now, and I'm going to sell Joe's string of horses. Joe loved them, but I'm just not a horse person. And Donagin'll need rehab. You've been wonderful taking care of him, and you love him. I don't know how his injury will turn out, but however it does, you'll be the best home he could have. And don't worry about the vet bills. I'll cover them."

"But Elsa!" I protested. "He's like … he's a valuable animal. One of the nicest horses I know. And the vet says he'll come back. Even with his injury, you could probably—"

"No. My mind is made up. If you don't want him, I can try to sell him, I suppose, but I really, really want you to have him, unless that's not what you want."

I hesitated. "Are you sure? Absolutely sure?"

"Of course, I'm sure. I've thought about it and it's the best thing for everyone. Say yes."

I exchanged glances with Cameron and he shrugged, a grin spreading over his face.

"Say yes," Elsa repeated.

"All right," I said at last. "Yes. And thank you. Thank you so very—"

"Good!" Elsa interrupted, her voice brisk. "That's done, then. I'll email you the papers tomorrow. I've already had them drawn up. A simple transfer of ownership. Remember, you're doing me a favor. Don't back out on me."

"I won't," I said meekly. I tried not to feel as if the universe had just done something very, very strange, but I couldn't help it.

"All right," Elsa was all business now. "Check your email and let me know if you have any questions. I'll sign off. Bye!"

The line went dead. I turned and looked at my husband. "Well," he said. "That was ... interesting."

"Yes." It was all I could say. Donagin. I couldn't believe it. Esther as a dressage mount, and Donagin my jumper? It was staggering to think about.

"Well, come on," Cameron said, gesturing toward the door. "Let's go do those chores."

We walked out to the barn, hand in hand. *Our place*, I thought. *The horses. My dream.*

It would come together. It *was* coming together. The account balances would stabilize, Donagin would heal, horses and people would move in.

And next year? *The people showing at the KHE Special better look out,* I thought. *We're coming.*

About the Author

Loraine J. Hudson lives and writes in a small town in Michigan. She loves oldies rock music, stained glass, digging in her garden, playing with her dogs, horseback riding and, of course, writing. She is often at her most creative when she is taking her retired racehorse out for an amble through the woods.

Using her pen name, Judith Wade, she has also created a series of youth/YA chapter books that incorporate a little bit of fantasy and adventure.

Visit her at:
- http://facebook.com/authorlorainehudson
- http://amazon.com/author/lorainehudson

or email *ljhwrites@gmail.com*.

Made in the USA
Monee, IL
25 September 2024

65871804R00085